Zacchaeus Wolfe

Major Zacchaeus Wolfe returns from the Civil War with the intention of leading a peaceful life. But the bitterness of past conflicts will not die.

His efforts to settle into his ranch are disrupted by a vengeance-seeking woman who wants retribution for the killing of her sons. Whilst in prison, awaiting trial for his alleged crimes, his family are attacked. Unable to help them he bides his time until the opportunity to escape arises.

Now the Gray Wolf will administer his own brand of justice and expect nothing but death.

Doncaster
Metropolitan Borough Council

DONCASTER LIBRARY AND INFORMATION SERVICES

Please return/renew this item by the last date shown.
Thank you for using your library.

InPress 2594

Zacchaeus Wolfe

P. McCormac

A Black Horse Western

ROBERT HALE · LONDON

© P. McCormac 2007
First published in Great Britain 2007

ISBN 978-0-7090-8243-9

Robert Hale Limited
Clerkenwell House
Clerkenwell Green
London EC1R 0HT

The right of P. McCormac to be identified as
author of this work has been asserted by him
in accordance with the Copyright, Designs and
Patents Act 1988

Typeset by
Derek Doyle & Associates, Shaw Heath
Printed and bound in Great Britain by
Antony Rowe Limited, Wiltshire

1

Conway the trader sat by the fire and waited in trepidation as he listened to the hoof-beats. He had pulled his wagon into the trees and found a clearing where he had lit his fire in the hope that no one would see the smoke and come to investigate. It was not that Conway was an unsociable man – far from it. He was a trader and used to dealing with the high and low of the land. It was just that these were troubled times.

The War Between the States had rumbled on, disrupting trade. But worse than the economic woes visited on business were the bands of militia roaming the countryside.

The disruption of the war had been an opportunity for ruthless men to take to the highways and prey on the law-abiding. Under the guise of patriotism they claimed it was their duty to ferret out traitors and deserters. In truth it was an opportunity for bands of vicious rogues to prey on the weak.

So Conway sat by his fire, anxiety making his hands tremble as he waited for the mysterious rider to pass by. The thing he feared happened. The hoofbeats slowed and stopped. He listened as the rider followed the tracks of his wagon into the wood.

The horse was a big black stallion. Maybe because of

the huge size and girth of the stallion the man atop looked slight. Conway stared in consternation, his anxiety heightened by the unexpected encounter. The rider had the reins gripped in both hands. He held the leathers high up against his chest well away from the ebony-handled pistol strapped to his body. The hands, like every thing about the man, looked undersized and delicate. They reminded Conway of nothing more than bright pale birds, restrained from flying aloft only by the leather reins.

The man rode into the clearing and sat his mount, not looking at the trader. His eyes were fixed on the fire. Conway shivered. He felt dwarfed by the huge presence of the stallion and its rider. For no reason he could think of the trader thought of the rider as a horseman of the Apocalypse. The man dismounted. He walked to the fire and held his hands out to the flames.

'Howdy, fella, my name's Conway. It's good to have company on a lonesome night like this.'

'Zacchaeus Wolfe. The fire brought me in.'

The trader's terror increased. His mouth dried up as he tried to fit the name to the man sitting opposite. Zacchaeus Wolfe, the legend, was sitting at the camp-fire of a harmless and terrified trader.

'Tell your wife to come into the fire. The night is cold. She must be very uncomfortable out there.' The man spoke without looking up from his contemplation of the fire.

The shaking in the trader's limbs was quite visible now. 'I ... it ...' he stuttered, then resigning himself to the inevitable, he called, 'Lena, come out of there.'

A young woman and a little girl emerged from the trees. The older girl was about fifteen and the younger aged seven or eight. The child ran to her father and he put a comforting arm around her.

'These are my daughters, Lena and Tracey.'

6

Wolfe nodded to the girls and a fleeting smile, seen only for a brief moment and easily missed, flitted across the man's forbidding features. Several days' beard added to the sinister appearance. Deep furrows were etched each side of his nose to meet with similar deep creases slanting along the side of his face. It was a lean face honed in planes and slants and carved in mahogany. The eyes were deep-set and brooding as if the man was forever looking inwards at some deep hell within himself. It was the face of a man who had witnessed the horrors of war and now directed his gaze within as if the nightmare of reality was too bitter to contemplate.

'I mean you and your family no harm.' The voice sounded weary.

'I was about to cook a meal, won't you join us?'

'That would be most kind of you. It would be a rare treat to eat with civilized folk.'

Conway continued his preparations for the meal, oddly reassured by the man's calm manner and matter-of-fact sentiments. A pot had been heating on the fire and the trader took out a well-worn wooden board and began chopping up the ingredients. Onions, potatoes, carrots, and fresh-picked mushrooms were diced and shredded and added to the stew.

'Are you a soldier?'

Conway had been so engrossed in his preparations he had not noticed his daughter approach the dreadful stranger.

'Tracey!' he called in alarm. 'Go and sit with your sister.'

The older girl was sitting near the fire with her chin in her hands, covertly watching the strange man. The legend raised his arm in placation.

'I do not mind, Mr Conway. It is natural for the young to be curious.' He turned his gaze to the young girl standing beside him. Something in him softened and his face did not seem so harsh in the dim light filtering down through the trees. 'Yes, I am a soldier, or at least I was a soldier.'

'Did you kill anybody?'

'Tracey!' In his agitation Conway stood and the chopping-board he was using fell unheeded to the grass.

A shadow crossed that hard face, visible only for a split second and then gone as if it had never been. But by now Conway had come round, taken his daughter by the arm and was moving her to safety beside her sister.

'I'm truly sorry, Mr Wolfe. She didn't mean to offend you.'

'Mr Wolfe,' the girl squealed, 'are you the big bad wolf?' She clapped her hands in delight.

Conway turned his horrified eyes towards his unwanted guest as if he expected fire to blast from those cavernous eyes along with a mouthful of curses. But the man was quietly staring down at his boots. Nervously Conway went back to his cooking. As he sprinkled salt into the pot his hand was shaking so badly most of his precious condiment went into the fire, igniting quietly in tiny blue flashes.

'Mr Big Bad Wolfe.'

His daughter was irrepressible. Before Conway could open his mouth to reprimand her she continued. 'Do you know the story of the Big Bad Wolf?'

The man with the terrible name shook his head. 'No, but I'm sure you do.'

The girl was venturing nearer to her listener. Conway ached to reach out and pluck his daughter from the alarming, dangerous man but he was helpless to do so for fear of offending his guest. Instead he put all his attention on tending his stew.

'Would you like me to tell it to you.'

The man stared bemused at the little girl and she took this as an invitation.

'Once upon a time. . . .'

Conway watched with trepidation as he saw his daughter take one of those delicate hands in hers. She stared earnestly into those deep pools of hell that had witnessed so much killing, and narrated her tale.

Zacchaeus Wolfe was a legend throughout the states. Appointed by General Lee to organize a guerrilla band that was capable of operating behind enemy lines, the Grey Wolves became feared and hated wherever they rode. They spread terror and destruction in the hinterlands of the Northern armies. The Northern command became so incensed at the wanton devastation inflicted by this small band of raiders that a massive reward was offered for the capture of their leader.

So notorious did the Wolves become that this same leader entered into folklore. Mothers everywhere would threaten their children with him.

'If you don't behave yourself Zacchaeus Wolfe will come in the night and get you.'

Yet here he was sitting by Conway's fire, and while he waited for his meal an eight-year-old girl held his hand and chattered to him as she would to a favourite uncle. Then Conway almost swooned.

'Then mummy pig said to the three little pigs, if you don't build a good strong house then Zacchaeus Wolfe will come in the night and eat you all up.'

Zacchaeus Wolfe's face softened. A faint smile took some of the sternness from his expression. Before the leader of the Grey Wolves could say anything the trader tried to distract him from his daughter's indiscretions.

'Stew's ready,' he croaked.

2

'My, I ain't ate a meal like that since I left home.' Zacchaeus Wolfe put down his tin plate and sat back with a contented sigh. 'You sure know your onions. I'd forgotten there were so many different kinds of things you could put in stew. How'd you come by them?'

'Conway shrugged. 'Well, I am a trader, I trade a little there and a little here.'

The two girls were clearing up after the meal. Zacchaeus Wolfe fished out a Durham sack and offered it to Conway. The trader held up his hand.

'Hold there, I got something a bit better than that.'

He went to the wagon and returned with two fat cigars and presented one to his guest. Somehow the tension had eased and the terror the trader had felt had dissipated. The fearful legend was sitting at ease by Conway's campfire like any other traveller.

'You're a lucky man, trader,' Wolfe observed as he inhaled cigar smoke with obvious pleasure. 'You have two lovely daughters there. Must make you real proud.'

'Oh, I don't know. They're more a credit to their mother.' The trader was silent as he drew on his smoke. 'She died two winters ago. I do my best but they could do with a mother's gentle touch.'

The men sat contentedly smoking while the girls chattered as they completed their chores. As he smoked

Conway took note of the man opposite. He figured Wolfe was aged in his mid-forties. Or maybe he was not so old. The hard school of war could sometimes age a man far beyond his natural age. He took note of the uniform, or the remnants of a uniform, that the man wore.

Grey, he decided. Travel-stained and creased, the uniform had seen better days. The man's black slouch-hat was dusty and almost as grey as was the tattered uniform. The only thing that had been lovingly cared for was the Army Colt in the leather holster, the butt facing forward and seeming a natural part of the man. Conway could see the gun was polished and gleaming. He shuddered to think how many men had died under the fire from that fearful weapon. But right now all that seemed far away as he sat by a fire smoking with his guest and listening to the cheerful chatter of his daughters. Then he started again as he heard the horses on the road. He waited to hear them pass but, like his present visitor now sitting by the fire the horses stopped, then the trader heard them enter the wood and search them out.

Conway glanced nervously at his visitor. The man seemed unconcerned. Casually the trader's guest rose and stepped to the far side of the fire so he faced the oncoming riders. He positioned himself beside the two girls and appeared to be staring into the trees, his eyes not looking directly into the fire. Serenely he stood beside Conway's daughters and drew on his cigar, to all intents and purposes a member of the family.

The riders made no greeting as they crowded into the clearing – hawk-eyes taking in everything. They were all very young, not one of them beyond his twenties. Indeed two of them looked as if they should have been still in school. There was a lean, hungry look about them, like a pack of animals that had tracked down their quarry and now gathered for the final kill. A blond, handsome young-

11

ster with cold, blue eyes stared speculatively at the group.

'Deserters,' he stated then wound his reins around his saddle horn and with graceful agility slid to the ground. 'You know what happens to deserters?'

Conway blanched. 'You got it all wrong, mister, I'm a trader.'

'Deserters.' The young man ignored Conway's protests. 'What do we do with deserters?'

The question was directed over his shoulder to the young men behind him still sitting their horses, and all the while he was watching the two girls. They stood nervously before the horsemen like frightened deer cornered by the huntsman.

'Why, we hang them, Brother Elmer,' came the chorus. 'Deserters are traitors.'

'This is nonsense,' protested Conway. 'I was exempted from army service because of ill-health.'

'I can smell deserters from five mile away. My nose tells me you are deserters. That rebel has still got on his uniform.'

'The war is over, friend.' Zacchaeus Wolfe spoke softly. 'Lee surrendered at Appomattox. Go back to your head-quarters. Your job as hangmen no longer exists. An amnesty was declared for all who register.'

The youngster tipped back his hat, exposing dirty, blond hair. His handsome face creased into a smile. He had perfect white teeth adding to his clean-cut, good looks.

'Listen, old man, we're going to hang you and this fat geezer here. We'll spare the females for they'll provide my brothers with some sport. My brothers are young and need to be acquainted with the joys of the flesh.'

The quartet of men on the horses whooped with delight.

'Elmer, me first, before Demetrius,' one of the young-sters called.

Conway was aghast. He stepped up to the young blond man so callously deciding the fate of his family.

'For heaven's sake, this is all a dreadful mistake. These are my daughters – they are but children. Has the war made you so hard that you have no pity? I have money and trade goods. Take those if you must have something, and leave us in peace.'

For answer the youngster backhanded the trader across the face. Conway staggered back under the blow.

'Father,' screamed the little girl. She would have run to his side, only an arm reached out and restrained her.

'Stay with your sister,' Zacchaeus Wolfe said softly to her and she stepped back, her eyes wide with fear. Lena put a comforting arm around her. Again he spoke, the voice soft as if he was still addressing the little girl. 'I suggest you get on your horse and take your boys back to your headquarters and find out what orders they have for you. These people are innocent travellers. There is no need for you to molest them. Just mount up and go.'

And Elmer laughed. It was a low, mirthless laugh – a laugh of a young man who had never met anything in his short life that caused him to doubt his own capabilities to meet all obstacles and overcome them. It was a laugh of a confident young man with four armed men to back up his claims.

'Old man, you are a coward and a deserter. We have met many such on our patrols. We decorate the trees with their stinking bodies as a warning to other draft-dodgers and deserters. We carry out this task because we get a bounty for every lily-livered coward we hang and also because we enjoy our work. But enough of talk.' Elmer turned slightly to his brothers while at the same time reaching for his holstered pistols. 'Let's get to it, boys.'

The man on the other side of the fire reached up behind his neck. There was an almost imperceptible movement and something flickered across the firelight. The blond man made a choking sound. He put his hand to his throat. A small steel handle had appeared in his neck. He opened his mouth and made strangled, gurgling noises. His companions were in the act of dismounting. They paused and stared with some bewilderment at their leader.

Elmer pawed at his neck. Crimson froth was bubbling from his mouth and the hand at his throat was suddenly dark with blood. Slowly he sank to the ground still making those horrible gasping noises. His brothers were bewildered. The next to the leader in age – a tall, blond youth, leapt to the ground and ran to his brother. He examined the wound in his neck. The man was convulsing and it was evident to all he was dying.

'Goddamn it, he's been stabbed,' the youngster yelled in panic. At the same time he twisted round to stare at the man by the fire. 'You done this, you murdering bastard.' He went for his gun.

The ebony-handled gun in Zacchaeus Wolfe's holster seemed to grow into his hand and flame belched from the nozzle. The youngster's head was snatched back as the bullet entered his forehead and exited, carrying with it most of the back of his skull. As he flopped back to lie beside his dying brother his hand had not yet managed to pull his weapon.

The thunderous explosion of the Colt set the horses to plunging and rearing. One of the brothers had managed to dismount before the panic. He was raising his pistol to sight on the stranger when that deadly weapon spoke again. He staggered back as his eye suddenly disappeared and a bloody spout of brain and blood spewed from the back of his head. Then he too joined his brothers in the mould of the forest clearing.

The two youngsters who had remained mounted

managed to calm their horses. They stared in frightened horror at their brothers sprawled in death. Then they looked with some fear and hatred at the slight figure standing by the fire.

'There is no need for further bloodshed. If you do as I tell you can live.'

The boys made no reply, only staring in boiling hatred at the man who with such terrible efficiency had wiped out their companions.

'Remove those Winchesters and toss them to the ground. Then unbuckle the gunbelts and let them fall also.' While the boys were complying with these instructions Zacchaeus Wolfe walked across to his first victim and, stooping, withdrew a thin blade from the dead man's throat. As he wiped the blood on Elmer's jacket he spoke again. 'Now pack your brethren back on their horses and tie them on.'

It took some time for the youngsters to carry out the instructions. The boys struggled with the weight of their older brothers. Conway made a movement as if to assist but a gesture from Zacchaeus Wolfe halted him.

'Go from this place. I shall follow behind to see you do not turn back and harm these people.'

Leading the horses with their dreadful burdens the youngsters rode away. When they thought they were safely out of range they turned in their saddles.

'We'll kill you for this, old man. We'll track you down some night and you won't die easy.'

Zacchaeus Wolfe gave no hint he heard the threat hurled at him.

'I would advise you to pack up and leave this place, trader. They may have friends they can call on to come back and try and exact revenge. Best they do not find you or your family.'

'They would have killed us and ravished these children but for you.'

15

'Trader, I regret the killing, but you are right. Men like that have no conscience. They are too cowardly to volunteer for active service. They form little bands of so-called militia and terrorize the countryside. Thankfully, now the war is over so too will the necessity for such vermin to find legitimacy.'

In a short time the clearing was empty and silence once more descended. The ashes of the camp-fire were the only testimony that men had passed this way at all. There was nothing to indicate that three young men had died so violently. Ancient leaf-mould soaked up the spilled blood and the forest reverted to its own eternal peace.

3

'Bother Zacchaeus.' The Reverend Makepeace Wolfe greeted his brother without any hint of warmth in his voice. 'So, the prodigal returns to his family.' The eyes took in the frayed uniform, the gun hanging on the hip and the gaunt face.

Makepeace was the elder of the brothers and had become a minister of the church. In contrast to his brother's lean, muscular build his jowls had filled out, as had his waistline. His hair had receded slightly and his lips had thinned from preaching against the seven deadly sins.

'Who is it, Father?' A dark-haired young woman thrust her head past her father's shoulder and stared for a moment at the newcomer. 'Uncle Zac, is it you? Oh, Uncle Zac.' Then she hurled herself past the preacher and flung her arms around the travel-stained Zacchaeus.

'Lavinia,' her father spoke sternly to his daughter, 'try and act with some decorum.'

'But Uncle Zac,' Lavinia said, leaving off her hugging only to drag her uncle up the steps and inside the house. Makepeace Wolfe was left to follow after – a look of displeasure on his austere features.

'Oh, Uncle Zac, it's so good to have you home again. Lucius and the boys should be home soon too. Isn't it wonderful the war's over! Oh, listen to me chatter on. You must be wore out after your journey. Have you had breakfast yet? I'll get you something to eat. What would you like? I could do you an omelette. I make an absolutely divine omelette.'

If his brother's reception had been cold his niece's welcome certainly made up for it in warmth and effusion.

'Now you go and wash and change your clothes. Then come right down to the kitchen. Over breakfast you're going to tell me all about yourself and what you did during the war. Lucius wrote to tell me you were famous. He said you were promoted to major. Imagine Major Wolfe – and Lucius is a captain. Oh, I'm so excited. Do hurry back down to breakfast, Uncle Zac.'

After breakfast the brothers sat in the preacher's study and an uneasy silence ensued. After the gushing welcome of his niece the awkwardness of his brother in his presence made the returning warrior distinctly uncomfortable. During the war Zacchaeus Wolfe had commanded men and killed men but he found his brother's stern demeanour difficult to cope with.

'Ahem.' Makepeace cleared his throat preparatory to speaking. 'It is good to see you came through the war safely. My sons will be returning soon. I have to ask what you intend to do now. There are certain reports of your reputation that have preceded you. Reports, I must say, that are distressing in the extreme. You seem to have taken our surname and made it a thing to be feared.'

'Do you mind if I smoke, Makepeace?'

'If you must smoke I'd rather you did it outside. I will not have the sins of rough men brought into my home.'

Zacchaeus sighed. 'As you will, Makepeace. I had hoped to put the past few years behind me. I chose to fight for a cause I believed in. You are a man of God and you chose the path of peace. I was just a simple rancher. Now I wish to return to that life. I take it the ranch is still in the family name?'

'With my duties as pastor I have not been able to tend

to the farm. Some of the old slaves – I mean servants – have stayed on and tried to keep the place going, but I'm afraid the place is run down. If you intend to make it a going concern it will take a lot of work and dedication.'

'I guess I'll ride out there and take a look for myself. Do you want to accompany me?'

'Brother Zacchaeus, there is something weighing on my mind that must be brought out in the open. As you just admitted, you are a man of violence whereas I am a man of peace. I have never been able to comprehend your willingness to fight and I suppose I never shall. My sons went off to this war because they were conscripted. I tried to keep them at home but the state was obdurate. My prayers and pleas were of no avail. I need to extract a promise from you, Zacchaeus. I want you to kneel down now with me and pray with me. Will you pray for forgiveness for the terrible sins you have committed in the past.'

For long moments Zacchaeus Wolfe stared at his brother, then he nodded. 'I have done and seen things that no man should ever have been subjected to. Long ago I gave up believing in a just God. Some of my actions I regret, some I thought were justified but, Brother Makepeace, I will kneel and pray with you if you think it will do any good.'

'It grieves me to hear you express those sentiments, Zacchaeus. Every day of the war I prayed for my family. My four boys went to the war against my wishes. God listened to my prayers and now they are to be returned safely.' The pastor bowed his head and prayed in a deep solemn voice. 'Lord, You have delivered my brother Zacchaeus home safely from the perils of war. In the next few days. You will also bring home my boys, Lucius, Quinton, Marty and Murdock. We will be reunited again as a family. Let the bloodletting cease. This land has had enough blood poured out upon it. Our young men have been sacrificed on the altar of war. May all men of violence hang up the sword and take up the ploughshare in its place.'

When Makepeace fell silent Zacchaeus looked at his brother for some hint that the praying had ended. When none was forthcoming he said, 'Amen' out loud and waited.

'Zacchaeus, will you swear to give up your violent ways?'

Zacchaeus looked with surprise at his brother.

'I beg of you to hang up your guns and lead a peaceable life from now on. My boys look up to you. In their letters home they were full of admiration for your deeds and the adulation of young men for their uncle who has become a hero to them. Tell me now you will do as I say and never use your weapons to take life ever again. I am afraid that they will want to emulate you and commit deeds of which I will be ashamed. Will you do this for me, Zacchaeus?

The two men, both still on their knees stared across the few feet that separated them.

'If this is dear to your heart, Makepeace, then I will do as you wish.'

'Swear, Zacchaeus, this is the family Bible.' The pastor handed to his brother a book with a well-worn black-leather cover. 'Swear on the family Bible.'

Not taking his gaze off the pastor the warrior with the deep unfathomable eyes put out his hand – that graceful hand that had killed countless times in a war of countless dead – and forswore his life of violence.

'I, Zacchaeus Wolfe, swear on the family Bible held by my brother, the Reverend Makepeace Wolfe, that from this day henceforth this hand will never pull a weapon on another fellow-being. As God and Reverend Makepeace Wolfe are my witness.'

Makepeace Wolfe stood, raised his brother from his knees and put his arms around him. There were tears in the pastor's eyes as he embraced his brother for the first time since their childhood days.

They heard the commotion outside the house and the then the excited squeals of Lavinia mixed with a chorus of male voices.

'I have a feeling our family is complete now, brother. My sons are returned from the war.'

4

Zacchaeus Wolfe cocked his head and listened to the gunshots coming out of the hills. He pursed his lips and shook his head, then stood back and looked down the lines of fencing he had been erecting for the past couple of weeks. The fence-posts ran straight and true and he nodded in satisfaction. The shooting had ceased. Zacchaeus went on working at his fence.

'Uncle Zac, Uncle Zac.' Someone was calling from the road. He had noticed the buggy for some time. Now he looked up and saw his niece, Lavinia, waving frantically with one hand while holding on to her hat with the other. A young man was in the driving-seat. Zacchaeus threw down his sledge and began walking down to the road.

'Oh, Uncle Zac, you must meet Barnabas. Barnabas this is my Uncle Zac.'

Zacchaeus nodded and took in the young man sitting beside his niece. He had a good, square face with a wide, generous mouth. Barnabas took off his hat and nodded nervously to Zacchaeus.

'Howdy, Mr Wolfe, it sure is a pleasure to meet you.'

'Howdy, Barnabas. I'm afraid I'm the only one here to greet you for the time being. The boys are up in the hills hunting. They'll be back when they catch something or when they get tired of shooting at shadows.'

The young man pushed back his hat and stared up at the hills. 'I sure wish I'd known they was going hunting. I bet there's plenty of game up in them there hills.'

'I don't think so. The Bluebellies came through here and burned and pillaged on the way. Left the people with nothing. They had to hunt and scavenge those hills to survive.'

The young man coloured and looked down at his boots. Lavinia smiled nervously.

'Barnabas is from Illinois.'

There was an awkward silence and Zacchaeus realized the youngster had probably fought on the opposite side during the war.

'Mighty fine place by all accounts. What brings you all this way to Virginia?'

'My brother is a director of South West Railroad. He sent me ahead to survey a route for his railroad.' Barnabas smiled suddenly. 'Lucky for me, 'cause I got to meet Miss Lavinia here.'

'Well, Barnabas, if I can hitch a lift up to the house I'll take a break from fence-building and play host to you young 'uns.'

Shortly they were all sitting on the veranda of a somewhat lavish house that had been very run down during the years that Zacchaeus Wolfe had been away at the wars. He was explaining to Barnabas and Lavinia his plans for the ranch. Suddenly there was loud whooping and shouting mixed in with the sound of hoofs as four horses came racing up the road.

'Looks like your brothers must have smelt the lemonade,' Zacchaeus remarked as he watched the youngsters pull up in the yard, making the quiet scene hideous with the din of the famous Rebel yells. When they saw the visitors they piled down from their mounts and swarmed up onto the veranda.

'Sis, you sure pretty up this place with your visits.'

'Howdy, fella. You sweet on our Lavinia?'

'You marry our sister you marry us as well. We'll eat and drink you out of house and home.'

'You have to beat us all at wrestling to win our sister.'

For several moments there was pandemonium as the boys larked around teasing an embarrassed Lavinia and her beau. Zacchaeus Wolfe sat in the midst of the adolescent high spirits and smiled quietly as he observed his nephews.

Lucius was the eldest, with dark curly hair and a long, lean face. His younger brothers were dark-haired also. Quinton, the youngest, had dark brooding eyes, a straight nose and wide firm lips. Next in line was Marty with elfin good looks and mischievous eyes. In contrast Murdock his twin was fair-haired. He was growing a beard that he kept trimmed to the area round his lips and chin. It gave him a pensive and serious look. Eventually the brothers quietened down enough to turn to their uncle.

'Uncle Zac, we brung you a present,' Lucius said with a broad grin on his handsome features.

Zacchaeus pursed his lips and nodded. 'Sure would like to see that, Lucius. No one ever brung me no present out of no hills before.'

The boys looked at each other and burst out laughing. Marty turned and unhooked a sack from his saddle. It was heavy and something moved as if alive. The youngster carried it to his uncle.

'Careful, Uncle, it might bite.'

A rank smell of fear and animal musk came from the sack. The boys watched eagerly as their uncle gingerly undid the draw. Carefully he parted the opening but a fraction. For long moments he stared at the frightened eyes peering up at him.

'Where the hell did you find this?'

'Shot his ma. We reckon it was her as was taking the calves from the top pasture. Won't take no more. Found this little tyke in the den.'

Zacchaeus Wolfe looked up at the ring of eager faces watching him and he smiled at their expectant faces.

'Sure is mighty thoughtful of you, boys. What the hell am I supposed to do with a wolf cub?'

5

Zacchaeus Wolfe rode into town when he received the summons from his brother. He was surprised to find the whole family gathered in the parlour. An additional guest was Barnabas, looking sheepish beside a glowing Lavinia.

'Brother Zacchaeus, welcome. I thought it best we all met together for this. It is an important event and as you are uncle to my children I feel obliged to include you.'

'Oh, Uncle Zac.' Lavinia jumped up and flung her arms around her uncle. He smiled warmly at his niece.

'Well, what is this important occasion I been invited to participate in?' He half-guessed already why he had been summoned.

Lavinia turned and nodded her head at Barnabas. The young man stood up, his square, honest face an agony of embarrassment.

'It's like this, Mr Wolfe. I asked the Reverend Wolfe if he would have any objections to me marrying Lavinia. . . .'

Zacchaeus was not sure which of the boys snorted as he tried to hold down his mirth but it set the others off. He tried to suppress a smile himself and only just succeeded in remaining poker-faced as Barnabas stumbled on.

'Reverend Wolfe said as I was to ask your permission as well, for you were as much father to his children as he was.'

Zacchaeus nodded as solemnly as he could. In spite of

or because of the frowns their father was directing at them the strangled noises of mirth from the boys was beginning to run out of control.

'Well, Barnabas, I feel honoured on two fronts. Firstly I feel honoured that Lavinia is to be betrothed to such a fine young man. Secondly I feel obliged to my brother for including me in this little ceremony. You certainly do have my blessing. I feel certain she will be in good hands and I wish you and her all happiness. When do you two reckon to tie the knot?'

Lavinia had moved to be at the side of Barnabas. She was looking with real happiness at her beau.

'I'm still surveying for the railroad. When my brother arrives I hope to tell him about Lavinia and ask his blessing on our marriage. After that it can't be soon enough for me.'

By now the boys were almost hysterical. Reverend Wolfe stood, a severe frown on his face.

'I must apologize for the rude behaviour of the rest of my family. I sincerely hope it does not give you second thoughts about marrying into this family. I assure you I will lecture them severely about their ill-mannered conduct.'

As he rode back to the farm Zacchaeus smiled to himself as he remembered the boys' youthful hilarity. He cut across to the top pastures and came across Seth, the former black slave but now a waged freedman working on the fencing. Seth waved a hand as he looked up from his work. He removed an old felt hat and wiped at his forehead with a coloured kerchief.

'Howdy, Master Wolfe. Sure a hot day for working.'

'We got ourselves a lifetime job replacing all that fencing.'

Soldiers on both sides of the conflict had plundered farms on their marches. Fencing was a favourite target for kindling as was livestock for food. Zacchaeus, with the

27

help of his nephews, was combing the hills for steers. They were beginning to collect a tidy herd, but because of the years of neglect the cattle had reverted to the wild and had to be fenced in, otherwise they would have returned to their wild habitat.

'Why don't you have a break and come up the house for some lemonade?'

Seth's wife, Angelina, an attractive young mulatto, served up a jug of lemonade.

'Join us, Angelina. Sit a while and drink with us.'

The woman looked uncertainly at Zacchaeus but perched on the edge of a cane chair. Seth was a good-looking, young black man with broad shoulders and brawny arms. He had been with the Wolfe family as a boy and had been purchased along with three other youngsters.

Isaiah Wolfe, Zac's father, had been a humanitarian and saw no reason not to treat his slaves as human beings. As a result they had felt no compulsion to run when the war came. They had stayed on and tried to keep the farm as best they could when the white men had been called to active duty.

'What you hope to do with that animal you got penned up out in the yard?' Seth asked as he sipped at the sweet liquor his wife was so adept at providing.

Zacchaeus took his hat off, put it on the table and picked up his lemonade. 'Danged if I know, Seth. My nephews gave it me as a present. So I feel sorta obliged to keep him. I been trying to tame it some. I figure on sitting in his cage with him every day while I feed him. That way he should get used to me.'

'They boys sure mischievous. I reckon the war put a wildness in them.'

Zac grinned, thinking of poor Barnabas trying to put forward his proposal of marriage while his future brothers-in-law chortled at his discomfiture. 'I don't think the war had anything to do with it. They're just young and full of tomfoolery. They'll be along presently to work.'

They looked up as a horseman came riding up to the yard. It was Tobias, another of Zacchaeus's black cowboys.

'Would you look at you all sitting there at ease while this poor little ol' slave does all the work,' he jibed. Tobias was a skinny cowboy with long legs dangling well below his horse's belly.

'How you doing up there, Tobias?'

'Got another half-dozen head combed out of the rough, Mr Wolfe.' The cowhand dismounted and came up to the veranda. 'Used my lariat to corral them in a blind. Could do with some help to bring them down to the bottom pastures.'

'Good work, Tobias, have yourself a drink of lemonade. My nephews will be here soon and we'll take some of them along to help. Seth is doing such a good job on that fencing I wouldn't like to take him off it.'

'Oh, yeah, I could do with some help too,' moaned Seth. 'I guess I was born under a unlucky star.'

'A lazy star if you ask me,' countered Tobias, helping himself to large glass of lemonade.

They rode up into the hills with Quinton, Marty and Murdock. Lucius had volunteered to help Seth with the fence-building. Tobias was in the lead, guiding them to the captured steers. As they approached the blind where the cowhand had gathered the cattle a bunch of riders appeared up above them on a low hill.

Zacchaeus squinted up at the horsemen. He counted five and wondered what they were doing on his ranch. The riders spotted Zacchaeus and his crew, and angled their mounts towards them. He waited patiently as they approached. A wide-shouldered, handsome man with a goatee beard was in the lead. By his side was a very attractive woman with dark-red hair.

'Howdy,' the big man greeted Zacchaeus.

Zacchaeus nodded. 'Howdy.' He figured both the man and the woman were in their late thirties. Behind them were three other men. One was a narrow-eyed swarthy looking man in his early thirties. There was something tugging at Zacchaeus's memory as he looked at the remaining two riders. They were only youngsters, barely out of boyhood. Their unfriendly gaze roved over Zacchaeus and Tobias and the boys. Suddenly they stiffened and to Zacchaeus's consternation pulled pistols and aimed them at his party.

'It's him, Ma. That's the bastard as killed Elmer and Thadeus.'

6

Zacchaeus Wolfe had not been leader of the Grey Wolves for being slow to think and act. His ability to weigh up quickly and take advantage of every situation, no matter how daunting, had carried him successfully through the war. Even as the youngsters fired at him he plunged his spurs into the stallion. His mount lounged at the man and woman who had reined in before him. The big horse cannoned into the two and the woman screamed as she was thrown to the ground. Her companion was cursing and trying to control his badly frightened horse.

Zacchaeus was past them and in between the two youngsters who, because of his quick movement, were unsighted with their handguns after firing off their first fusillade. His fist lashed out and the one on his left was punched out of the saddle. He gathered his legs under him and launched himself at the gunman on his right. The youngster yelled out in fright as he was hurled to the ground with Zacchaeus on top. Even as they fell he had gripped the boy's revolver and ripped it from his grasp. Still on the ground and with a swift movement the boy was hauled on top of him with a wiry hand gripping his throat in an iron grip.

Shielded from any fire by his captive the Colt was pointed at the most dangerous of the gang. The swarthy man had his weapon out and was aiming at Zacchaeus

31

from the top of his horse. He hesitated as he saw the Colt in Zacchaeus's hand. Zacchaeus held his fire – just keeping the revolver pointed at the man on the horse.

'Enough, enough! That's enough! Aaron, put up that gun and you also, Demetrius!' The man with the goatee beard had regained control of his horse and was now in the process of imposing the same control over his men. 'Aaron, see to Tamara!'

Reluctantly the swarthy Aaron holstered his revolver. Without taking his eyes off Zacchaeus he dismounted. With smouldering eyes Demetrius grudgingly put up his weapon.

Still keeping a grip on the throat of his captive Zacchaeus stood and hauled the frightened youngster to his feet. He kept the captured Colt loosely aimed towards Aaron. Instinctively he put the man down as the most dangerous of the party. He said nothing as he watched, awaiting developments.

'I'm sorry about this, mister. It was unforgivable, this unprovoked attack on your party. These boys are young and wild. Their part in the war unsettled them.'

Demetrius and Aaron were in deep consultation with the woman. From time to time she looked at Zacchaeus. He could read nothing from her expression. He had not released his hold on his hostage.

'Uncle Zac, Uncle Zac, it's Quinton, he's been hit.'

Everyone turned to the source of the voice. The boys along with Tobias were dismounted and gathered round a figure on the ground.

The leader of the band turned to Zacchaeus. 'See to your man. I'll keep my boys under control.'

Zacchaeus pushed his captive roughly from him. His victim stared sourly after him, rubbing his throat where Zacchaeus's inflexible grip had been strangling him. For all the man's reassurances Zacchaeus retained the captured Colt and made sure he did not turn his back on the group clustered around the woman. His eyes were bleak as he strode to where his nephew lay.

The boy lay in the grass, his head pillowed by a rolled-up slicker. His face was ghastly pale. Blood was staining the front of his shirt. Zacchaeus knelt and gently opened the bloody garment. A dark hole was discernible almost dead centre. Blood was weeping continuously. Quickly Zacchaeus unwound his bandanna, folded it neatly and pressed it gently against the hole. Quinton's eyes opened. He stared up at his uncle through pain-clouded eyes.

'Uncle Zac, is it bad?'

'Not too bad, Quinton. Tobias, get back to the house. Bring back a rig. We'll need to get Quinton to town. He'll need to be seen by the doctor. Marty, hold this pad in place.' He stroked the wounded boy's face. His heart was filled with dread. He had seen enough wounded men to know this was a serious injury.

When he stood he was facing the little group of strangers who had accosted them. In his hand he still grasped the Colt he had taken from his attackers. For a moment he trembled as the rage surged through him. Then he felt the familiar killing coldness settle on him. His senses sharpened. Every movement around him registered – every twitch of limb – every shift of eye. Sounds were magnified. He heard birds call to each other in the hills. Colours were stark as his mind became concentrated on the danger. He almost brought the gun up. His finger ached on the trigger.

'*I, Zacchaeus Wolfe, swear on this Bible held by my brother, the Reverend Makepeace Wolfe, that from this day henceforth this hand will never pull a weapon on another fellow-being. As God and Reverend Makepeace Wolfe are my witness.*'

Slowly the tension eased. The chill of the killing madness subsided. Once more he became mortal. He could almost hear the angel of death sigh and the beat of his wings as he passed overhead. He stared out at the five strangers. Behind him he heard Tobias leave for the ranch house.

'Mister, I sure am sorry for this deed.' The man with the goatee had climbed from his horse. 'How bad is he?'

'We'll have take him to town to be attended to. It looks serious enough.'

'If there is anything we can do to make up to you for this? I feel sure an awful mistake had been made. The boys mistook you for someone else and started shooting. Their elder brothers were slain in the war and they mistook you for the killer.'

'Mister, you are trespassing on my land. Gather your people together and ride away. If I ever see any of you on Wolfe property again I'll shoot without warning just as you did. Is that clear?'

Zacchaeus's voice was cold and toneless. He watched as they mounted up. The two boys were glaring with undisguised hatred at him while their companion Aaron eyed him up speculatively. The woman smiled at him in an attempt to break the tension.

'Mr Wolfe, there has been a terrible mistake. I am the boys' mother. They believed you were responsible for their brothers' slaying. Whatever the truth of the matter, I have told them to be let bygones be bygones. Terrible things happen in war. Men are not responsible for matters that are sometimes beyond their control. Can we put this behind us and move on? We have only just arrived in the area and I do not want this business to sour any encounters we might have in the future.'

Zacchaeus stared bleakly up at her. For long moments she held his gaze, then broke the contact and looked across at her consort. The man moved up to Zacchaeus and held out his hand.

34

'Name's Samuel Eldridge, I want to pay any medical bills for the wounded man. You can find me in town. We've hired a house there – 36, Patterson Avenue. Please call and see me in the near future.'

Zacchaeus ignored the outstretched hand.

'Eldridge, you anything to Barnabas Eldridge, the railroad surveyor?'

'My brother, you know him?'

Instead of answering Zacchaeus raised the Colt he had taken from the boys. Out of the corner of his eye he saw the man Aaron stiffen and his hand go to his holstered weapon. Zacchaeus ignored him. He rotated the cylinder and ejected the bullets allowing them to drop to the ground. With a swift movement he flung the gun far up the hill.

'Get off my land, Eldridge, and take your brats with you.'

'I understand your feelings, Mr Wolfe. I probably would feel the same if someone rode up and gunned down one of my men.' He swung on to his horse. 'My offer still stands. I will pay any medical bills and I would welcome you to visit my house.'

They rode away with the gunman Aaron keeping a wary eye on the lone man standing watching them go.

'Uncle Zac.' Murdoch's quavering voice came to him as he stood there trembling and the tension drained from him. 'Uncle Zac, I think Quinton's stopped breathing.'

7

'I do not believe there is any greater pain in this sad vale of tears than for a father to bury his children.' As the Reverend Makepeace Wolfe spoke his voice quivered with emotion. The little group of mourners stood with bowed heads in the graveyard. Balanced on the wooden slats above the newly dug hole the polished wood of the coffin was beaded with glistening raindrops.

'I buried Quinton's mother ten years ago. I never thought then that I would be burying my son before I joined her. I would that it were me in that coffin. It is not right and fitting that a son should go to the grave before a parent. However I must bow to the will of the Lord. The Lord giveth and the Lord taketh away.'

The funeral party retired to the Reverend Makepeace's house. The boys were subdued and Lavinia red-eyed from weeping. Barnabas stayed by her side, protective arm around her shoulder. Zacchaeus stood uneasy and silent. Barnabas and Lavinia approached him.

'Mr Wolfe, I have had words with my brother about the killing. The boys who fired the shots are the sons of the woman under his protection. She is Mrs Tamara Prothero and her sons are Demetrius and Keiren Prothero. They were under the impression that you were responsible for killing their brothers. I have made my feelings clear. I have told Samuel the killing of Quinton was unlawful and the ones responsible should be tried for it. I'm afraid he didn't agree with me. Said the killing was an accident and that no further action would be taken.'

Zacchaeus stared at the youth. 'Have you told my brother Makepeace this?'

'No, I was hoping you might tell him for me. You can appreciate my position. I desire to marry Lavinia and now my brother shelters the people responsible for killing Quinton. Mr Wolfe, I can't tell you how angry I was when Samuel told me of his intentions to protect those people. I'm afraid I said some harsh things to him. To make matters worse, he has told me on no account must I marry Lavinia.'

Zacchaeus nodded sombrely.

'There is more to this, Mr Wolfe. My brother said he was considering prosecuting you for the murder of the elder Protheros. Mr Wolfe, I am telling you all this by way of a warning. Samuel is a powerful man. He is a personal friend of the governor. If he does as he threatens he could make sure you are imprisoned or even hanged for the killings.'

'Your brother must do as he thinks fit.'

'Mr Wolfe, I will do all in my power to help you. I too have friends in high places. Some of the men I served in the war with are now in eminent positions. I will petition them for your immunity.'

'Thank you, Barnabas, I appreciate your efforts to help.'

The youth looked miserable. 'I do not believe all this stems from Samuel alone. That Prothero woman influences him. It is she who drives this thing forward. Any mischief will come from her and those evil sons of hers.'

'My, my, Barnabas, those is strong sentiments coming from you.'

'You do not know them as I do. The whole family are

malicious and vicious. I rue the day my brother fell under the spell of that Lady Macbeth. And Aaron, their companion, is a sadistic killer. My brother has fallen into a nest of vipers. He is in as much danger as this family is from their scheming and plotting but he is blinded by the charms of Mrs Tamara Prothero.'

When Zacchaeus told Makepeace of all Barnabas's concerns the preacher was quiet for so long he thought there would be no response. Eventually his brother looked up at Zacchaeus.

'Zacchaeus, we must reconcile ourselves to these people. I will call on Samuel Eldridge and offer peace. I will ask Lavinia and Barnabas to accompany me. You'd better stay out at the farm. Don't come into town no matter what. This feud must cease now before more blood flows.'

As he left the town, Zacchaeus Wolfe's ruminations about recent events were deep and troubled. On drawing near the farm he was puzzled by the large number of horses he could see gathered on the approach road. He was even more perplexed to see they were cavalry mounts and that a troop of the United States Cavalry seemed to have descended on his farm.

As he pulled into the yard he could see no sign of the soldiers had presumably arrived on the horses now tethered out on the road. Slowly he dismounted and led his horse towards the stables, preparatory to unsaddling.

The soldiers inside the barn were standing in a semicircle. There were six of them and they were aiming their standard issue Winchesters at Zacchaeus. For a moment he stood very still, observing them.

'Don't make any sudden moves, Major Wolfe. We can all hit what we aim at.'

Zacchaeus drove a clenched fist into the haunch of his mount and at the same time yelled at the top of his voice.

The horse leapt forward, scattering the soldiers. Zacchaeus was running for the house. He had almost reached the porch when he saw more soldiers in the doorway. Shots whistled overhead and then even more men in uniform emerged from around the corner of the house.

'Don't try anything, Wolfe,' someone yelled. 'We'll gun you down.'

More and more soldiers were coming into view. He stopped dead then. The leader of the Grey Wolves had fought Bluebellies during the war. But then he had fought them on equal terms. He was usually mounted and well-armed, with the backing of his own soldiers. Alone and surprised he was no match for a troop of United States Cavalry. He stood there waiting while the soldiers circled warily. Every gun in view was aimed at the lone figure in the yard. He noticed rifle barrels poking from the windows of his house.

'I was under the impression the war was over. Seems you fellas haven't heard the good news,' he remarked laconically. 'I'm just a poor rancher trying to make a living. I ain't broke no laws.'

'Get his gun.'

One of the soldiers approached from behind. Zacchaeus felt an explosion of pain in the back of his head as the man swung his rifle. He pitched forward into the dirt of the yard.

'I ain't taking any chances with this wolf. Keep your guns on him while I frisk him.'

Zacchaeus felt hands on his body as the soldier searched in vain for the non-existent weapons.

'Well,' an exultant voice called out, 'we caught the wolf without his teeth. Clean as a whistle, he is.'

'Get them manacles. Sooner he's shackled the sooner I'll be easy.'

He felt his hands dragged above his head and the jingle

of chain. The iron bands were clamped around his wrists. His feet were next and then he was rolled over on to his back while a chain was attached between the hand-constraints and the shackles on his feet.

'Get him up.'

Rough hands dragged him to his feet. It was then he discovered the chain between his hand-shackles and ankles was so short it prevented him from standing upright.

'Put him on his horse.'

They dragged him on the horse and used more chains to attach him to the saddle. He felt the wetness trickle from the wound in the back of his head. Unable to move or ease his limbs for the weight of chains they had used to secure him he began the painful journey back into town.

8

'Good news then, the army have arrested Wolfe.' Aaron, the swarthy-faced gunman was slouched indolently on a chair with his arm draped casually over the rear support when he made this remark.

'That's the leader of the pack caged. I am going to cause him a lot more grief than he ever caused me when he killed my children. Now we move in on his cubs while he languishes in prison unable to do a thing about it.' Tamara Prothero had a flawless skin, which, along with her dark-red hair, gave her an aura of eternal youthfulness. 'He will hear about their ruin but be unable to do anything about it. His helplessness will drive him mad. He will go to the gallows knowing he has paid in the blood of his family for the murder of my sons.'

'What about Barnabas?' Aaron asked. 'He would do us harm given half a chance.'

Demetrius was cleaning his nails with a Bowie. He looked up from his task. 'I can take care of him. Given half a chance I'd stick him with this here.' He held up the Bowie and gazed lovingly at the keen blade.

'No,' snapped his mother. 'His demise must not be traced to us. I can't jeopardize my position with Samuel.'

'I'll look after his girlfriend,' offered her other son, Keiren. He stretched out luxuriously on the *chaise-longue*, 'Oh, Lavinia, just one look from those dark eyes sets my blood on fire.'

41

Tamora looked fondly at her sons. 'Perhaps there is a way to enjoy her and get rid of Barnabas at the same time.'

The three men in the room looked at her expectantly.

'Barnabas and Samuel go hunting with the Wolfe family tomorrow. That old reverend fool has organized it in an effort to make peace with Samuel. Let's put our heads together. Just think of it – the Wolfe boys in the hills with Barnabas – that little minx Lavinia waiting back at the house alone. . . .' Her voice trailed off and her lips twitched in a sardonic smile.

Patchy clouds flitted across an otherwise clear sky as the little hunting party set out from the Wolfe farm, leaving Lavinia waving a cheery goodbye from the porch. The only one missing from the party was the eldest boy, Lucius. He had ridden north to engage the services of a lawyer for his Uncle Zac, incarcerated in the army prison with a murder charge hanging over him.

'This is just like old times,' Samuel remarked to his brother, 'when we used to go hunting with Pa.'

Barnabas smiled back at his elder brother. 'You always got the best pot. I guess I was too young to compete with you.'

'Well, today is your chance to beat me, young Barnabas,' replied the brother. He squinted up into the hills. 'Why don't we split up?' He turned to the Wolfe boys. 'I'll make a circuit of that hill. There's a wooded valley behind there that might yield some deer.'

The Reverend Wolfe nodded in agreement. 'Good idea, I'll go with you, Samuel, and guide you to the most likely spots.'

'Sounds OK to me, Reverend. You boys take Barnabas there and hold his hand. Maybe you can find a tame rabbit for him to shoot.' With a wave Samuel set off on a trajectory from the rest of the party with Makepeace leading the way.

'He's an arrogant fool,' muttered Murdock as he watched Samuel depart. 'Tell you what, Barnabas, what if Marty and myself work our way round ahead of you. We can drive any game towards you.' He looked speculatively at his prospective brother-in-law. 'You can shoot that thing?'

Barnabas touched the stock of his hunting-rifle and grinned at the boys. 'Don't you worry about me. I can shoot all right.'

The hunting party split up and began searching the hills for their quarry. None of the hunters were aware that hostile eyes were watching them from the hills and they themselves were the targets in a different kind of game.

Lavinia was so engrossed in her baking she had not heard the horse arrive in the yard till the loud knocking on the front door alerted her. She wondered why Angelina, the black girl who looked after the domestic chores and cooking, had not answered the door but then remembered she had taken a dinner-pail to her husband, Seth, working somewhere out on the ranch. She wiped her hands on a towel and went to the door.

'Oh, thank God you're here, Lavinia. There's been an accident. It's Barnabas, he's been hurt in a hunting mishap.'

Lavinia stared at the tall, beautiful woman with some misgivings. She had been introduced to her at Samuel's house but got the impression the woman did not like her. At the time this had not bothered her much, for Barnabas had voiced his own dislike of Tamara and of her unsettling influence on his brother. These thoughts flitted through her mind as she tried to take in what the older woman was telling her. Then the meaning of her words registered. Her hand flew to her mouth.

'Barnabas, oh no! How bad?'

Tamara's eyes slid away as if unable to face telling the girl of the seriousness of the incident. 'I . . . it looks pretty bad. I don't know about these things. I sent my boy Demetrius for the doctor. But he keeps calling for you. Oh God, I feel so helpless. Can you possibly come?'

'Of course. Give me a minute to saddle up. Should I bring anything with me?'

Tamara was shaking her head. 'Just come and hurry. I'm so afraid.'

They rode hard for the hills. As they travelled Tamara filled in Lavinia with some details.

'Somehow Barnabas got caught in the crossfire from the guns. They were stalking on foot. Oh, Lavinia, I hope we are not too late.'

The woman's words were designed to upset Lavinia and they had the desired effect. Lavinia rode with dread in her heart. She had lost a brother from gunfire and now it looked as if her betrothed was lying direly wounded somewhere in the hills.

Aaron paced along parallel with his quarry. He had the higher ground and he could easily follow and even anticipate Barnabas's moves. His mount was tethered well up in the hills and he had no worries about finding it when he needed it. Barnabas rode easily, his eyes scanning his surroundings.

The Wolfe ranch was a mixture of hilly country, unsuitable for crops but used to graze cattle, and flatlands that were ideal for growing corn or cotton and tobacco. Before the war it had been a prosperous ranch with an extensive herd of cattle and well-tended fields. With the passage of two armies at various times through the county the fencing needed to separate crops from farm animals had all but disappeared. The dried wood used in the construction of fences was irresistible to the soldiers as a source of

44

kindling and for constructing shelters. The animals had been slaughtered to feed starving troops.

Zacchaeus Wolfe, having sworn an oath to his brother to abstain from violence, had been attempting to restore the farm when he had been abruptly arrested and taken in chains to the army barracks in Salem. Now his two faithful ranch hands struggled as they had in the past to carry on without him.

Aaron waited under a large tree, his rifle held indolently at a slant with the barrel resting on his knee. He observed Barnabas as the youth approached. Seeing the figure beneath the tree Barnabas reined in and stared at the gunman. Aaron smiled in greeting, exposing a row of gold-capped teeth. He was well aware of the youth's dislike of him.

'Shot anything yet, Barnabas?'

'Not yet, we've only just started. What are you doing here?'

'I'm hunting too.'

'You weren't invited to the hunt as far as I remember.'

'No.' Aaron's face twisted up into a wry grimace. 'I invited myself.'

For a long moment Barnabas studied the swarthy features of Aaron. He had heard something of his reputation as a gunman. It was rumour he had fled Kansas for murdering disbanded Confederate soldiers. It said a lot for the authorities now in control that he was not pursued for his crimes with any enthusiasm.

'I'd advise you to make yourself scarce. The Wolfe boys are up ahead somewhere. In view of what happened to their brother Quinton they might not take too kindly to you trespassing.'

Aaron nodded soberly. 'They still sore about that? Maybe in a way it was justifiable killing. Their uncle had killed three members of the Prothero family. There's an old Biblical saying, an eye for an eye.'

Barnabas eyed the gunman coldly. 'Nothing justifies the killing of a young man like that. Now, get the hell out of here. Go back to that she-cat Tamara. You and she are well matched.'

Aaron was slowly nodding his head. 'I thought you might be like this. Tamara isn't bad. She would be friends with you if you'd let her.'

'If she gives up this stupid vendetta against the Wolfe family I might be persuaded to believe there is some good in her. I see her hand in the arrest of Zacchaeus.'

'Very shrewd of you, Barnabas. Tamara persuaded your brother to approach his friend, the commander of the Union troops in Salem. He asked for Zacchaeus to be taken into custody and placed on trial for the murder of Tamara's sons. He'll hang for his crimes.'

Barnabas stared aghast at the gunman. 'Samuel used his influence to have Zacchaeus arrested! That woman is indeed evil.'

'She asked me to give you something.'

'There's nothing I want of her, only a promise to leave Virginia and take her ill-bred whelps with her.'

The rifle came up and was pointing at the youth on the horse.

'She sent this.' As he spoke Aaron fired.

The shot at such close range hit Barnabas in the chest. His horse jumped and he fell across the neck of the animal, his face buried in the mane. The terrified horse took off with the mortally wounded man still on itis back.

9

Lavinia was familiar with the line shack situated well up in the hills. As a little girl she had once or twice visited it when out on excursions. She remembered sheltering inside with her brothers from a sudden storm.

'Luckily we found this cabin and were able to carry Barnabas here.' Tamara said as they pulled up outside.

The horses were winded, for the last part of the climb had a very steep gradient. Lavinia slid from her pony, her anxiety showing in her face as she waited for the older woman.

'You go ahead, Lavinia, I'll take care of the horses.'

Lavinia gave the older woman a strained smile. She mounted the single step to the cabin door and disappeared inside. Tamara took her time tethering the ponies before following.

Inside she found a white-faced Lavinia standing facing her two sons.

'What is the meaning of this, Tamara? I asked this pair where Barnabas was and they just laughed. What sort of trick are you playing on me?'

Tamara laughed. 'No trick, my dear Lavinia. My sons desire you. Take a look at them. Aren't they fine young men? I had four such fine sons – excellent boys like these. Now I have but two, for your Uncle Zacchaeus killed my first-born and my next eldest, along with their cousin.'

47

Lavinia frowned at her. 'Whatever happened in the war is not my concern. I'm sure many dreadful deeds were committed. The war is over now. We must forgive and forget.'

'Never!' The word was said with such venom that Lavinia stepped back a pace from the contorted face of Tamara. 'If you knew the grief and anguish I have endured at the thought of my boys murdered by that butcher. He is in prison and while he languishes there he will see his family taken from him one by one. Perhaps then he might just begin to imagine the suffering I have gone through. And then, when he is the last of the Wolfe family, when he is broken by grief I will watch him hang.

'Already he has lost one nephew. Now on this day his niece will give pleasure to my sons. It is little enough compensation for the death of my boys.'

'What are you saying? Don't you know I am to marry Barnabas?'

'It won't be a wedding, I'm afraid, but a funeral you'll attend with Barnabas. I brought you here on the pretext that your fiancé was injured. I have every confidence that he now lies dead in the hills below. It was Aaron's task to take care of that little chore. I ride now from here to meet him and we will lay the blame on your brothers. They have every motive to kill Barnabas out of revenge for the killing of Quinton, their brother. It will give me great pleasure to see them hang for a murder they did not commit. Then at a suitable time, Aaron will pick a fight with your brother Lucius and Aaron will kill him, for he is a skilled gunman. There is no one to match him in cunning and fighting skills. Now I must go. This day I begin the breaking of Zacchaeus Wolfe.'

Tamara smiled at her sons. They stood there watching Lavinia with wide grins on their faces.

'Enjoy her, my sons. I will leave you to the feast.'

As she turned to the door Lavinia started forward. 'For God's sake, woman, have you no pity!'

She got no further for a pair of strong arms encircled her and Demetrius buried his face in her hair. He moaned loudly and his brother burst out into an insane cackle.

'Don't do this. What have I ever done to you?' Lavinia pleaded.

Tamara turned back and stared at the anguished face of the young girl. 'What have you done? I tell you what you have done. You have done nothing to deserve this. My sons were innocent also. What pity did Zacchaeus Wolfe have when he gunned down my Elmer. Well, I extend you the same pity.' She turned her back on the trio and pulled open the door of the cabin. As she slammed it behind her she heard an anguished shriek from inside and the excited laughter of her sons. She smiled a satisfied smile.

'Where are you now, Zacchaeus Wolfe? Where are you now when your niece needs you so desperately?'

As she swung on to the pony there was another desperate scream from inside the cabin. This time it was the woman spurring away down the incline who laughed.

The Reverend Makepeace Wolfe heard the hoofs galloping somewhere below them. He turned in the saddle and looked curiously towards the sound. Up ahead Samuel had dismounted and was scanning the woods. He carried his hunting-rifle at the ready, confident he had seen movement within the trees. There was no doubt within his mind that a deer or some such creature was lurking within the wood waiting for a chance to make a dash for safety. So when the hoof-beats disturbed the quiet he turned and frowned in the direction of the noise.

'Goddamn it, what a racket! They'll frighten everything within earshot.'

With his companion he watched the trail and then

caught sight of the roan running with the rider huddled across the horse's neck.

'Hell's bells, who's that?'

Reverend Wolfe frowned slightly at the mild swearing. 'I can't tell from here. The rider looks as if he's in trouble. If we ride hard down the other side we can cut him off.'

Without waiting for a reply Makepeace urged his horse forward and began the race to head off the rider.

Samuel swore again. 'Bloody hunting gone to hell,' he muttered savagely and fumbled to get his rifle into the scabbard. Then he swung on to the saddle. Still muttering he urged his mount after the preacher who by this time had disappeared down the side of the hill. Part-way down the slope he could see the runaway horse and Makepeace yards behind in full pursuit.

Slowly Makepeace Wolfe drew alongside the panicked horse. The rider's identity was hidden from him for the face was buried in the mane of the horse. He edged ahead and began the tedious process of slowing down the fleeing horse. With infinite patience he forced his mount into the path of the runaway. His tactics worked. The other mount shied away to the side of the path and pulled up. Makepeace hauled his horse alongside and grabbed the loose reins. The man on the horse made no indication he was aware of what was happening. Makepeace dismounted and held both horses captive while he waited for his companion to catch up.

Samuel jumped down and ran to the other side of the captured horse.

'Barnabas,' he yelled. 'My God, there's blood everywhere!'

Together they lifted the unconscious man from his horse and laid him on the side of the track. The youth's shirt was a crimson mess of blood. Makepeace grabbed the loose horses, dragged them off the track and secured them in the trees. Then he came and knelt beside the brothers.

'He's still breathing. It looks like he's been shot.'

Makepeace pulled off his jacket, folded it into a pillow and placed it under the wounded man's head.

'Barnabas, can you hear me?'

The boy lay with chalky face, making no response. Makepeace bent his head and put his ear close to the boy's mouth. He raised his eyebrows. 'He's still breathing but only just.' The preacher began to examine the blood-soaked shirt. 'It looks as if he has lost a lot of blood. There must have been some sort of accident.'

They heard hoofs pounding down the trail towards them.

'That'll be my boys, Marty and Murdock. We'll have to send for help. I'll try and stop the bleeding. But my heart quails within me. It looks a grievous wound.'

'Dear God. Barnabas, my brother, don't die on me.'

Two riders pulled up. Their horses were breathing hard.

'Tamara, Aaron, what the hell you doing here?'

'Oh, Samuel, we saw it, we saw it all,' Tamara was clambering from her horse. Aaron stared at the little group showing no expression.

'How is he, is he dead?' The woman's face was a filled with dread.

'He's still breathing but only just. You said you seen it. What the hell happened?'

Tamara dropped to her knees beside the wounded man. She reached out and caressed his face. 'Oh, Barnabas, so young, oh dear God, so young.'

'What happened, Tamara? You said you saw it.'

When she looked at him there were tears streaming down her cheeks. 'The Wolfe boys . . . Aaron and I saw it all. They turned their guns on him and shot him. We were too far away to do anything. We could see he was griev-ously wounded. We followed to see if there was any help we could give.' She turned her tear-streaked face to the preacher. 'Your boys, Reverend, they shot poor Samuel's brother in cold blood. He never stood a chance.'

'You must be mistaken. My boys would never do such a thing. They are good, God-fearing boys brought up in a Christian household. There must be some mistake.'

'Ain't no mistaking it, Reverend. Mrs Prothero and myself saw it all. Your whelps gunned down this poor boy. It was out and out cold-blooded murder.'

Samuel turned a thunderous face to the preacher. 'Damn you, Wolfe, and damn your murdering family. Your brother murdered Tamara's children and now your sons have murdered my brother. They'll hang for this. I swear by all that's holy they'll hang.'

10

'What we gonna do now that Zacchaeus been taken to prison?'

'Hell I know, Tobias. I guess we just have to do what we been doing all during the war and carry on till he comes back.'

'What if he don't come back, Seth? The reverend he done looked after us while Zacchaeus was away at the war.'

The two black hired hands were standing in front of the Wolfe ranch house discussing the latest development. They had just learned that their boss was languishing in a military jail. Neither understood why Zacchaeus had been arrested.

'I thought the war was over and Zacchaeus was given an amnesty. He sure believed it was all behind him. That's why he was doing all this work. He was sure he could turn the ranch around and start making a profit. Damn white folk and their doings, I guess I'll never understand them.'

Seth grinned back at his friend. 'I'm sure they say the same thing about us.'

'Hell, Seth, I reckon we just do what we can till Zacchaeus return home. I'm going back up in them hills and comb out some more mavericks. It would be a welcome home for him if I increase his herd.'

'Yeah, just you be careful up there. Look what happen last time you went up, young Master Quinton he lying cold in his grave.' Seth shook his head, frowning. 'Poor Reverend Makepeace, his sons all come home safe and sound from the war and then his youngest boy is shot dead on his own farm. Ain't no way right.'

Tobias heaved his long frame on to his mount. 'I'll see you at supper. Tell Angelina I'll be real hungry after a day's wrangling.'

'Hell, Tobias, I hardly ever see my wife, she so busy in the kitchen cooking enough food to fill that belly of yours.'

Tobias grinned at his friend then wheeled his mount and rode out. In spite of his skinny frame he was a phenomenal worker and had a prodigious appetite.

He rode higher into the hills than usual, for his previous efforts at seeking out stray cattle had cleared most of the lower slopes. He was of the opinion he had probably exhausted the potential for fresh finds of strays but felt compelled to keep on trying.

His route took him near the vicinity of the old, deserted line shack. Tobias was quartering the area searching for signs of steers when he came upon the horse-tracks. He reined up and studied the hoof-prints. The cowboy could read sign better than most and he began to piece together what had happened.

At least four riders. He guided his pony alongside the tracks. *Two came in first and then two join them. One move out again then two leave some time later. No sign of the fourth rider going. That's strange.*

Warily he approached the old shack. It looked derelict and deserted as usual. For a while he studied the old building.

'Howdy, anyone at home?'

There was no response and he called again. He climbed down and examined the front of the shack. He noted the marks made by horses tethered to the hitching-rail. Inside

54

he stood and looked at the signs of disturbed dust and dirt. There had been a struggle of some sort for the few remaining sticks of furniture had been knocked about. Thoughtfully he walked outside and followed a single track where two sets of boot-prints showed that someone had led a horse around the side of the building and out into the hill. The boot-prints had returned without the horse. He followed the prints and they led right up to an old derelict mine-shaft.

Cautiously he peered inside. Someone had disturbed the boards that had blocked the entrance. Intrigued he began to pull at the slats and made an opening. Warily he slipped through.

There was a musty, dank smell within the mine entrance. Very little light filtered in from the opening he had made in the boards to enable him to step inside. He wished he had a light and fumbled out a small tin of matches. The tiny flame did not cast light very far and he had just gone a few steps when he kicked something. There was a tinny rattle and he looked down to find a lamp lying on the ground. He shook the container and was able to hear a faint sloshing sound. Then he cursed and dropped the burnt out match as the flame reached his fingers.

Damn.

When he had lit the lamp he shuffled forward. Then he smelt it. Cordite. Someone had recently fired a shot inside the mine.

What the hell's been going on here?

He came upon the horse first. There was congealed blood on its ear where the bullet had entered.

They shot the horse. Maybe it was injured and this saved a burial.

He was about to return when curiosity prompted him to explore beyond the horse's body. Not much further on there was something white and still sprawled on the floor of the mine. He held the lamp high and saw the body.

'Oh, dear Lord above, some poor woman has met her end here in this lonely place.'

He bent over the partly clothed body and gazed into the face, then straightened up suddenly. 'Miss Lavinia, this can't be true, not Miss Lavinia.' His hand trembled so violently he thought he might drop the lamp.

He knelt beside the body and an immense sadness overwhelmed him.

'I gotta bring you home, though it break Reverend Makepeace heart and your Uncle Zacchaeus too.'

There was a dark gaping wound in the girl's throat. For a moment Tobias considered what he should do.

'I'll carry you back to the cabin. It ain't right you lying here in this dark hole.' He removed his jacket and placed it over her shoulders. Then he gathered the girl in his arms and stood.

'This ain't right, missy. You should be cold and stiff.'

He put his head close to the girl's mouth and held his breath. The fine hairs in his ear stirred gently. Then he was running past the dead horse and out into the daylight, the desperate state of the girl giving him strength beyond normal.

Reverend Makepeace Wolfe sat on a high-backed wooden chair on the landing. An open Bible lay on his knees. He was reading from the holy book, his lips moving soundlessly as his eyes followed the text. It was the family Bible he had used when he requested his brother Zacchaeus to foreswear violence. The door to the bedroom opened and Doctor Langdon stepped out into the landing. Reverend Wolfe stared with tragic eyes at the doctor.

Doctor Langdon was a man in his forties. His hair was thin and wispy and brushed carelessly across the top of his scalp. An equally thin and wispy moustache adorned his upper lip. He was in his shirtsleeves with his coat slung across one arm while in his other hand he carried his medical bag. Carefully he turned and gently closed the bedroom door behind him. He walked the few short steps to the preacher.

'Reverend, I truly never saw such injuries inflicted on anyone and they survive. Your daughter is hovering between this world and the next. I have sewn the terrible wound in her throat but it is doubtful if she will ever speak. The vocal cords are damaged irreparably. It is surely a miracle she is still with us.' The doctor shrugged helplessly. 'She also sustained a grievous head injury. If the brain is damaged other functions may be impaired. Reverend Wolfe, I wish I could tell you better news.' The doctor put out his hand and rested it on the preacher's shoulder. 'I will call again tomorrow.'

'Thank you, Doctor. May I see her now?'

Doctor Langdon nodded and Makepeace rose to his feet.

'Reverend Wolfe, this has been a tragic day for you and your family. I heard the news that your boys were arrested for murder and now this. . . .' again the doctor shrugged helplessly. 'Zacchaeus is in prison also. If there is anything at all I can do please don't hesitate to ask.'

The preacher stood and nodded. He shuffled towards the bedroom door, his shoulders bowed under the terrible weight of his grief. Doctor Langdon watched him for a moment then turned and descended the stairs.

11

Outside the town limits a small band of horsemen gathered. They were mostly young men all aged under twenty. All had seen service in the Confederate army. All were armed with pistols and carbines. All had set determined faces.

Lucius Wolfe was their leader. He sat his horse and looked over his companions, his handsome oval face sombre. A dozen young men to take on a squadron of cavalry, he thought, and then brushed the thought aside.

'You all know what is expected of you?'

The young riders nodded. 'Sure, Lucius, we ride in and beat seven shades of shit out of them there Bluebellies.'

Lucius smiled at the speaker as did the rest of the assembled riders.

'George, you couldn't beat a carpet,' quipped one.

George, a narrow-faced youth with a drooping moustache pulled out a long-barrelled Colt revolver and waggled it above his head. 'I killed Yankees in the war and I reckon I still got me a full belt of bullets to kill me a few more.'

'Fellas, it ain't gonna be that easy. They may be expecting an attempt to rescue Marty and Murdock.'

'Hell, Lucius, we bin there before. There ain't one of us would want to be left out of this caper. They been kicking our folks off their farms and chivvying us young 'uns for too long now. A man can only take so much shit afore he turns and fights back. We're behind you one hundred per cent. Just you make sure you haul your brothers off them there gallows while we're killing them soldiers. As soon as we see you Wolfe boys safe we break off and ride out. Couldn't be simpler.'

Lucius wheeled his mount around. 'Let's go. We ride in separate. As soon as Marty and Murdock are on the gallows that's the signal.'

They watched him ride and in twos and threes at spaced intervals they followed.

The townspeople were gathering in little knots of sullen menace. They muttered amongst themselves and shot long looks of hate towards the troops guarding the jail. Workmen were still labouring on the high wooden structure being erected out front. Armed troops ringed the area. No one was allowed anywhere near the lock-up. Today the Wolfe boys were to be hanged for the murder of a Northerner. The townsfolk neither knew nor cared whether the boys were innocent or guilty of the murder. They resented the fact that a military court had tried the boys and pronounced sentence on them. Military rule did not sit easy on the shoulders of the people of West Virginia.

They had suffered during the war as the Federal Army had ravaged their communities, confiscating goods and food and livestock to feed the hated Bluebellies. Now in the aftermath of their defeat that same army imposed the rule of law.

In the wake of the army had come the shysters and land-sharks and dodgy speculators. The hated Northerners had swarmed in to take advantage of a defeated and bewildered populace. Because many of the newcomers carried their belongings in bags made of a carpetlike material they were dubbed carpetbaggers.

Farmers and smallholders were being forced to sell out at knockdown prices. Those who resisted endured raids by armed men. Barns were set alight and livestock slaughtered. Now the hated army was to hang the sons of a respected preacher. No wonder the air was alive with tension and resentment.

The workmen began packing away tools and clambered from the wooden gallows they had been building. They formed up with a little group of civilians who had been escorted to a privileged position to view the execution.

Samuel Eldridge and his paramour along with her sons and the gunman Aaron waited with some anticipation for the condemned men to appear.

For Tamara this was a pleasurable achievement in the waging of her vendetta against the Wolfe family. She would watch the nephews of her hated enemy Zacchaeus Wolfe kick and choke their way into the next world. It would not bring back her own boys but it would give her satisfaction that their uncle was languishing in prison helpless to do anything while his family was virtually wiped out.

When these boys were hanged it only remained for Aaron to kill Lucius and then wait for the execution of her enemy at the hands of the state. That was the event she awaited with avid anticipation. On that day she would gloat as Zacchaeus kicked out his life at the end of a rope. Only then would her lust for vengeance be satisfied.

The door of the gaol opened and soldiers appeared to form a guard. Colonel Benjamin Franklin emerged and paused to examine the wooden edifice on which he would execute his prisoners. He was heavily moustachioed and wore thick, bushy side-whiskers. The colonel was renowned among his men for being a stickler for discipline and order. He turned his head and issued an order to someone inside. Two more soldiers appeared followed by two civilians. An angry buzz arose from the crowd of onlookers as they caught sight of the Wolfe brothers.

The boys were escorted to the wooden steps that led to the platform of the scaffold. Their hands were manacled to the front and leg irons ensured they moved at but a shuffle. The soldiers guarding them nudged first Murdock, then Marty and indicated they were to mount the steps. Clumsily they climbed, their manacles and chains hindering any sudden movements. Using another set of steps more soldiers were climbing on to the scaffold. It took long painful moments for the party to assemble on the platform.

Using a ladder the soldier appointed as executioner fixed the ropes to the crossbeam. As the rope nooses dangled in front of the prisoners, for the first time they showed signs of agitation, stepping back a pace as the ropes appeared. Soldiers roughly pushed them back in place.

The crowd of civilians was growing restive. A rumble of anger could be heard. A few foul epithets were hurled at the ring of soldiers keeping the crowd at bay.

'Lieutenant, order the men to present arms. If there is any interference from the crowd they have permission to fire.'

The lieutenant duly passed on the order and the crowd grew more agitated as rifles were presented and pointed directly at them.

At that moment there was a disturbance behind the first row of onlookers. People were craning their heads around to see what was happening. A hush descended on the crowd and people fell back as a tall figure in a black frock-coat walked forward.

'Reverend Wolfe.' The name was whispered from mouth to mouth as he walked up to the line of soldiers. He stopped in front of a young recruit, the nozzle of whose weapon was almost touching the parson's jacket.

'Tell your commanding officer I have come to perform the last rites for my boys.'

The lieutenant stepped forward. 'Reverend Wolfe?'

'I am he.'

'Let the pastor through.'

The ring of steel was broken while Reverend Makepeace Wolfe entered, then it closed again behind him. Steadily he walked forward till he stood face to face with Colonel Franklin.

'I make one last appeal to your mercy. Pardon these innocent souls and show clemency towards the people of West Virginia. I will stand surety for my boys. They will remain within my jurisdiction till such time as you deem it safe for them to be released to lead a normal life.'

'Reverend Wolfe, much as I understand your pain and concern for your sons it is not within my power to release condemned prisoners. They must pay for their crime with the ultimate penalty.'

The preacher bowed his head for a moment. When he raised his face to the colonel tears were standing in his eyes. 'At least let me pray with them before you commit this heinous crime.'

Colonel Franklin nodded curtly and stepped aside. Makepeace Wolfe mounted the scaffold to minister to his sons. He embraced each one and then stepped to one side and opened his black leather Bible. It was the same book on which his brother had forsworn violence only a few weeks previous. He began to read aloud.

12

'Yip, yip, yip. . . .'

The unmistakeable Rebel yell echoed across the streets immediately followed by a fusillade of shots. There was a sudden explosion of men and horses out of side-streets and from down the main thoroughfare. Townspeople gathered to watch the hanging were suddenly caught in the crossfire of a major skirmish. It was as if the war had never come to an end as riders, blooded in the recent conflict, came riding out of nowhere to attack Federal forces.

These young men could ride and they could shoot and they could do both together. From every direction they came, guns flaming as they vented their anger and frustration on the occupying force.

In spite of Colonel Franklin's instructions to his recruits that they were to fire at any signs of resistance they were unprepared for the ferociousness and suddenness of the assault. Several of the soldiers were hit by incoming fire. As they fell, some screaming in pain, it panicked the young troops. They fired wildly without aiming as if they were still fighting conventional forces. Most of their bullets went wild and then the horses were among them, wheeling and squealing and adding to the noise and confusion. The young soldiers fell back. Officers screamed at the soldiers to form ranks and return fire. But the men kept falling back. Out of the mayhem and noise and smoke came Lucius Wolfe, riding the big black mare that had belonged to his Uncle Zacchaeus. Behind him trailed two riderless mounts.

They were intended for his brothers. He emptied his Colts into the troops around the scaffold. The survivors scattered to avoid the maddened beast bearing down upon them.

Reverend Makepeace Wolfe stood with hands upraised. In his hand was his Bible. He was shouting something but his words were lost in the general noise of firing guns and screaming men.

Lucius made it to the scaffold and hauled on the reins. The black obediently slid to a halt. All around him men were firing off weapons and riders were weaving through the ranks of confused soldiers.

'Murdock . . . Marty . . .' Lucius screamed, 'jump, for God's sake jump!'

The guards assigned to escort the prisoners on to the gallows were kneeling and firing into the milling horsemen. Seeing Lucius they turned their weapons on him. Murdock, loaded down with chains threw himself into the men crouching beside him. They fell in a confused tangle. Lucius discarded his empty Colts and pulled another from inside his jacket. As he did so he saw Marty felled by a rifle-swinging soldier. Coolly he shot the man as he was bringing that same rifle round to take a shot at himself. Then he saw his father.

Reverend Makepeace Wolfe was shaking his head vigorously at his son and waving his arms frantically. It was obvious to Lucius he was shocking his father with this rescue attempt. The preacher was a pacifist and had never witnessed such violence at first hand. Seeing his eldest son as an instrument of violence and killing was working against the precepts of his religious beliefs.

Thou shalt not kill, was one of the ten commandments handed down to generations of Christians and now his own family was engaged in breaking that precept. Makepeace Wolfe could not reconcile the killing of his own family and the slaying of the men who were carrying out that execution. As far as he was concerned the law of the land had pronounced judgment. Two wrongs did not make a right. And so he berated Lucius and attempted to warn him away.

For one awful moment of suspense father and son stared at each other. Then bullets began to hammer into the scaffold around Lucius. One of his spare mounts was hit and leapt high in the air, squealing and kicking at the sudden sting of the bullet. Lucius broke away from his father's frantic gaze and took in the state of this rescue attempt.

Murdock was lying with blood streaming from his head while the men he had struggled with were beginning to sort themselves out and readying their weapons to start firing again.

Marty also was lying supine beneath the ropes that were intended to strangle their lives away. With one last despairing glance at his father Lucius emptied his revolver into the soldiers atop the scaffold and spurred his mount away. Bullets were buzzing like hornets around him but miraculously he came out unscathed. A bugle called from somewhere and as suddenly as they came the attackers disengaged and swung their horses to take off into side-streets and away from the mayhem they had inflicted for that brief heroic moment.

They left behind their wounded and dead, for this was a battle they had not thought to win. It was but a sortie to aid an old comrade against the hated Yankee invaders. They rode out and scattered across the countryside. They knew the penalty for their actions. The harassment against them and their families would increase. Some of them would be forced to go on the run. Others would stay and fight on in a hopeless one-sided contest. They were but a ragtag gang of dissidents. The enemy was the combined might of the United States of America.

Colonel Franklin eventually brought some semblance of order to his demoralized forces. The dead were carted away. The wounded of both parties were shipped to the military hospital. Only after these matters were attended to could he return his attention to the original purpose of the morning's proceedings.

'Carry on, Lieutenant, the criminals must be hanged. This attack has not changed our purpose. Justice must be carried out.'

With the Reverend Wolfe reading in a shaky voice from his Bible, black hoods were produced and placed over the heads of his sons. Roughly the soldiers appointed as hangmen jerked the nooses down over the hooded heads. Any sympathy the guards might have felt for their young charges had been dissipated by the savage attack on their fellow soldiers. The guards stepped back and left the youngsters standing squarely on the twin trap-doors that would shortly be released from under them.

'Marty, at least Lucius believes in our innocence.'

'He did his best for us. It's a pity he hadn't Uncle Zac with him. If he'd been here we'd all be riding free now.'

'Maybe that's why they stuck him in a prison cell. More an' likely they shit scared of him. I sure hope he don't end up like us.'

'I'll see you on the other side, Murdock. Ma will be there to greet us.'

'I sure hope so, Marty.'

There came the rattle of a wooden lever and the boys dropped into space. The ropes tautened and jerked abruptly as the bodies came to the end of the slack. The chains securing their ankles and wrists jangled for a few moments as the condemned youths kicked their lives out, then there was nothing to be heard but the creaking of the straining ropes and the sobs of an old man mourning his deceased children.

Lucius had not been out to the ranch for some days for he had been seeking to bring some sort of legal redress for his Uncle Zacchaeus. His lawyer friend had promised to look into his uncle's case as soon as he was free to do so. Lucius then had to ride for home when he had learned of the fate of his brothers.

He had returned to Salem and went to see Samuel Eldridge to appeal for reasonableness and clemency with regard to the unlikely guilt of his brothers. Very quickly he had realized the hopelessness of his cause. In the face of Samuel's expressed venom and hatred for all the Wolfe family he had abandoned any hope of mercy from that quarter. Hence his abortive rescue attempt. Now he rode furiously for the ranch.

It was obvious he would have been seen and recognized during the attack. He had to go on the run. At the ranch he would be able to stock up on supplies. There had been contingency plans for such an event among the group of ex-soldiers he had recruited for the raid.

Right now he should have been riding with his brothers to freedom or at least a life on the run. Now he was riding alone and he had a bitter feeling of what his failed mission would mean. In spite of his efforts his brothers would most likely be hanged by now and he, Lucius, was the only Wolfe left to avenge the death of his brothers.

He was under no illusions about who had condemned Murdock and Marty to death.

'Samuel Eldridge, Tamara Prothero and her hellish whelps along with their pet gunman, Aaron.' He recited the names out loud as he rode. 'I swear vengeance on all that nightmare brood.'

He raised his eyes to the skies and wept tears of frustration and grief.

'Oh, that Uncle Zac were here. We would all be riding to freedom. He would not have botched that raid.'

There was more grief waiting for him at the ranch. Because of his absence on his errands of mercy he was still not aware of his sister Lavinia's plight.

13

Tamara gazed with some satisfaction at her two sons, Demetrius and Keiren. As usual Aaron sat with them, his swarthy countenance giving away nothing of his feelings.

'Our revenge for the murders of your brothers is proceeding nicely. Three of that devil Zacchaeus Wolfe's nephews are dead along with his niece. The remaining nephew is on the run with a price on his head.' She smiled with genuine pleasure. 'I have another wrinkle that should bring more grief to what remains of the Wolfe family. Recently I have been helping Samuel sort out his brother's belongings. I have been overseeing his documents regarding the route he surveyed for the railroad. The original plan avoided the Wolfe ranch and curved around the back of those hills. It did not take much persuasion on my part to point out to Samuel the advantages of the more direct route that would run through the Wolfe range.' She paused and waited for some reaction from her listeners.

'Hell, woman, did he fall for it?' Aaron was the only one to see the significance of Tamara's words.

'Absolutely. He takes heed of everything I say. He has instructed his agent to start the process of purchasing the Wolfe ranch. Then I put it in his mind to use existing regulations to buy the ranch at a fraction of the value. To do that the ranch must be vacant so we can claim the place is not being worked.' Tamara smiled sweetly at the gunman.

'That, Aaron, is your job. You ride out there and persuade everyone to move out of the house and chase off any workers who may be reluctant to leave. I don't care how it's done. Use violence if necessary. It is another twist of the screw for the evil bastard who murdered my sons. I want him to suffer the pangs of hell before they take him out to be hanged.'

'In view of all that has happened to that family, perhaps we shouldn't be too closely associated with that phase of the operation,' suggested Aaron. 'Why don't we persuade those Pinkerton men hired by South West Railroad to do the job for us?'

Tamara eyed him shrewdly for a moment before replying. Slowly she nodded her agreement. 'Perhaps you're right, the less we're seen around the Wolfe place the better until all this is over.' Her smile was filled with malevolence as she mulled over the ingenuity of her plan. 'My only regret is that I can't confront Zacchaeus Wolfe and tell him I am the instrument of all his sorrow and grief.'

Her two sons were gazing at their mother in adulation. 'Hell, Ma, this is better than just riding up to that old man and putting a bullet in his head,' opined Demetrius. 'But you're right. I want to tell him how much pleasure his niece Lavinia gave us before we slit her throat.'

The brothers eyed each other gleefully and laughed in fond memory of that incident while their mother gazed proudly at her two young sons.

'You have just given me an idea. Aaron, you say you are familiar with the sergeant in charge of the prisoners.'

'Yeah, he likes to play cards, so I fleece him a little each time. He can't stay away – thinks he'll recover his money in the next game.'

'Right. Here's the plan. Get him to inform Weolfe that his nephews are to be hanged but he overheard a deal that if he sends a signed confession admitting to the murder of my sons to the colonel he'll consider commuting the death penalty to a short jail sentence.'

'Hell, Ma, the Wolfe boys are already hanged. What good'll that do?'

Tamara laughed. 'That's just it. He confesses without knowing his nephews are dead. The pain of the loss is that much deeper. You think you can swing it, Aaron?'

'Sure, that sergeant is into me for a month's pay in advance. He'll do it all right.'

The cell was small, cold and damp. Every day Zacchaeus Wolfe stood and strained against his chains. He would lie on his back and holding the chains in his hands, would slowly straighten his legs while trying to resist the movement. At other times he would grip the bars of his cage and haul himself up using only the strength of his arms. Zacchaeus was not trying to escape. These exercises were just that – exercises to strengthen his body. Every day he performed them and every day he waited patiently to learn his fate. The rattle of the keys warned him of the approach of his jailers. He waited patiently for their arrival.

Sergeant McCluskey was a big Scotsman with a square, craggy face. He was as strong as an ox – with a brutal nature. His one weakness, as Aaron had discovered, was cards. Up till now he had taken no interest in his prisoner. His instructions were that he was to keep him manacled at all times, as he was considered too dangerous to be loose. McCluskey was slightly contemptuous of his superior's orders and could see no danger in the slightly built man in his charge.

'The higher powers have a proposition for you,' he informed the prisoner. He unlocked the cell door and walked inside, producing a folded paper and a pen. 'Your nephews are to be hanged in the morning, but if you sign a confession admitting to your killing of the Prothero brothers then the colonel will give them a prison sentence instead.'

If Zacchaeus had not spent the past weeks in chains in solitary confinement he might have probed further into this proposition. He was unable to communicate with the outside world. Through the prison grapevine he had learned of his nephews' plight. He had pondered long and hard how they had come to be imprisoned for murder. His instinct told him they were innocent. Long he had grieved over their probable fate. Presented with a possible means of securing their release even though it ensured his own execution, he did not hesitate. Without a word he took the writing-materials from McCluskey and wrote out a full confession.

McCluskey read over the declaration of his prisoner's guilt.

'You know this will hang you.'

The sergeant found it disconcerting to communicate with this manacled man, for he never responded in the usual manner. McCluskey's brutal treatment brought neither whinging nor cowering. Those black eyes just stared steadily at his tormentor and McCluskey always felt cheated that his victim did not plead for mercy. Those same calm, unfathomable eyes now stared back at him and with a curse the big sergeant swung around and left the cell.

Later when he presented the document to the colonel the officer was suitably impressed.

'Damn me, McCluskey, this will save us a lot of time and effort. Some big-shot lawyer has been making noises regarding our prisoner. It appears Wolfe's nephew engaged him before he made that attack on our forces during the hanging. This lawyer wants to see a proper trial.' Colonel Franklin looked up at his big sergeant. 'How the hell did you manage this?'

McCluskey shrugged. 'It's a natural gift I have with people. I win their trust with kindness. In the end they become so grateful to me they will do anything for me.'

Colonel Franklin looked doubtfully at the brute shape of the man standing in front of him. Somehow kindness was not a quality he would have attributed to him.

'Well, we'll get a trial organized straight away. With this confession it won't take long. We'll have another hanging. This time no civilians will be allowed anywhere near. I don't want a repeat of the last disaster.'

14

Fort Leander was now being used as part prison, part garrison for the troops assigned to impose order in West Virginia. It was rumoured that Jeff Davis was being held there but no one would confirm or deny this. Court was held in a large hall. A row of uniformed officers sat at a table and chairs and benches were arranged in rows like church pews. The benches were virtually empty. Only a few civilians were allowed in.

The lawyer who was to represent Zacchaeus Wolfe had petitioned Colonel Franklin for access to his client but this had been denied him. Now, for the first time he was to meet the defendant.

'This is most irregular,' he protested.

Theodore Lyman had interrupted his law practice when the war began. He had been a lieutenant-colonel during the war and met Lucius Wolfe when taken prisoner at Harpers Ferry. Lucius had befriended the enemy officer and helped in his exchange for Confederate officers. The lawyer was determined to repay the dept he felt he owed the young Confederate captain.

'I have not had a chance to confer with my client before this trial.'

'Don't worry, Mr Lyman, this won't take long. We have here a signed confession from the accused. He has stated here that he was indeed the person who shot and killed the Prothero brothers. Also we have the surviving brothers who witnessed the killing.'

Before the lawyer could make any reply his client was led into the court. He was heavily manacled. In spite of the circumstances he looked composed and at ease. Looking neither to right or left he was led to a chair and seated with two armed soldiers either side.

'May I see that confession?'

An orderly brought the document to Lyman. He read through it.

'Mr Wolfe, did you write this confession?'

'I did.'

'Can you tell me, what reason did you have to write it?'

'I was told my nephews would be spared from execution if I pleaded guilty and signed a confession.'

There was some agitation among the officers. Theodore Lyman stared hard at the self-appointed judges.

'We made no such promise.'

'I notice this document is dated the 17th, yet the Wolfe brothers were hanged two days previous to this date.'

For the first time Zacchaeus Wolfe stirred in his chair. He turned and stared at Theodore Lyman. 'They were hanged?'

'You were not aware, Mr Wolfe, that when you signed this confession your nephews were already dead.'

There was silence in the room as Zacchaeus Wolfe digested this information.

'No, I did not know,' he said at last.

'You took advantage of this man's loyalty to his family to extract a confession knowing full well that you had already hanged his nephews.' The lawyer's voice dripped with contempt.

'I tell you no such promise was made!' Colonel Franklin almost shouted the denial. 'The prisoner made the confession voluntarily.'

'Somehow, Colonel, I can't see Mr Wolfe suddenly confessing to a crime after repeatedly claiming his innocence. I can't see him getting a fair trial in this court. It is almost as if you were waging some sort of vendetta against this family. You are determined to execute this man after hanging his nephews. Is that because his sole remaining nephew made an abortive attempt to rescue his brothers from the gallows?'

'Mr Lyman, you are out of order. This man is a self-confessed killer. During the war there was a price on his head put there by the Northern Command.'

'I see.' Lyman's voice was icy cold. 'This trial is not about justice, it is about settling of scores for acts carried out during the war.'

'Damn you for your impudence!' Colonel Franklin was on his feet, his face red and furious-looking. 'There is no such agenda. The man committed murder therefore he must be hanged.'

'It appears you have already condemned the man. You have sentenced him before the trial even begins. My secretary here has made notes of all your prejudicial remarks. I shall be forwarding a report to the War Department and will ask for an enquiry to be conducted. I'm sure that even a colonel can't get away with meting out summary justice.'

Colonel Franklin's face took on an even deeper red colour – in fact it began to look purple. He opened and closed his mouth but no sound came out. An aide leaned over and whispered something. The colonel gripped the edge of the table and slowly asserted control. During this process the aide was talking urgently.

'Very well,' he finally grated, 'this trial is suspended. The prisoner will be transferred to Clarksville where he will stand trial for the murder of the Prothero brothers.'

Outside the fort a group of people were conferring.

'Damn that interfering lawyer, he's going to get that hellhound free.' Tamara's usually lovely face was distorted with fury. 'He'll smooth-talk them into letting him walk free. I just know it.'

'Can't we just kill the lawyer?' Demetrius asked naïvely. 'We could waylay him and cut his throat just like we did Lavinia.'

'No, damn it, it's one thing killing members of the Wolfe family but it might stir up something if a bigwig Northern lawyer is murdered. Samuel is already getting edgy after the Wolfe boys were hanged. It appears Lucius has issued threats against him and South West Railroad. He's declared his brothers were innocent and is accusing Samuel of their murder.'

'What are we to do?'

'There is one way to rid ourselves of the Grey Wolf.'

Tamara along with her two sons looked at Aaron. 'Go on,' she encouraged.

'Our friend Sergeant McCluskey.'

'What about him?'

'He's our man on the inside. Prisoners die in prison. Some hang themselves, some cut their wrists while others take poison and others are killed while attempting to escape.'

'What are you saying, Aaron?'

'I'm saying McCluskey can finish off our man. When he is being transferred to Clarksville, McCluskey can make sure he is on that duty. On the way Zacchaeus Wolfe can be killed while trying to escape. The army will not want bad publicity, especially after today. They'll just hush it up. In a week or two Zacchaeus Wolfe will be forgotten. Only us few and Sergeant McCluskey will know the truth.'

'You think McCluskey will do it?'

Aaron smiled his golden smile. 'If we pay him enough he will.'

15

'You want to be assigned to the duty of prisoner transfer?'

'Exactly sir.'

Captain Daniels looked at the big sergeant standing before him. The man was a veritable giant with large, scarred hands, evidence of innumerable fistfights. The face was craggy and that too showed signs of battle scars.

'Can I ask why you would want such a duty?'

'Well sir, I have been sergeant of the guard for some time and I could do with a change of scenery. A trip to Clarksville would do my morale the power of good. Also I've been watching that particular prisoner for some time and I think he is planning something.'

'You mean he'll attempt an escape?'

'I'm not sure, sir, but I did notice a change in him since his last court appearance. Before that he was calm and respectful now he's moody and resentful. I feel responsible for his safekeeping.'

'Very well, Sergeant. How many men would you require?'

'Just one sir, Corporal Greenalch and myself would be more than adequate to escort the prisoner to Clarksville.'

'Greenalch. If I remember correctly he's assigned to mess duties.'

'I know, sir, but Corporal Greenalch and me go back a long way. We joined up together and we're unbeatable in a scrap. And besides, sir, he wants to see Clarksville also.'

Captain Daniels signed the orders. Sergeant McCluskey

and Corporal Greenalch were to escort Zacchaeus Wolfe to Clarksville and hand him over to the military authorities to stand trial for the murder of Elmer Prothero, Thadeus Prothero and Lemuel Chambers, a cousin of the Prothero brothers.

In another part of town Samuel Eldridge was issuing orders of a different kind to the leader of the Pinkerton men hired by South West Railroad to protect mail trains and payrolls.

'You ride out in the morning to the Wolfe ranch and give them formal notice that South West Railroad have agreed to purchase the land now owned by the Wolfe family. Everything is signed and legal. Tell them there is no appeal against the compulsory order. The railroad must go through. It will benefit the whole region. Tell whoever you find out there that they have two days to vacate the premises. I'll leave the whole affair in your hands. By Friday I want the place empty. Understood?'

The Pinkerton hireling was a narrow-faced man with a week's growth of stubble on his face. He nodded at Samuel.

'I'll see to it, Mr Eldridge. Do you know who all's out there?'

'One of the owners is in prison. There is a brother, a Reverend Wolfe and he may be out there but he has a house in town. The son of the preacher, Lucius Wolfe, is on the run. It was him as created that mayhem that day when his brothers were hanged for murdering my brother. Other than that the only other people I know of who may be around are some black cowhands. So you won't need more'n a couple or three men to handle that.'

'I'll take care of it, Mr Eldridge,' the Pinkerton man said and tucked the documents he had been handed into an inside pocket. 'You can rest assured that ranch will be empty come the weekend.'

*

The cell door swung open and Sergeant McCluskey stood in the opening regarding his prisoner with some amusement.

'Well, Mr Big Bad Wolfe, it seems they have assigned me to make sure you get safely to Clarksville. For a time there I thought they were going to separate us.'

The big man moved inside the cell. He was swinging a bunch of keys in one hand. Zacchaeus Wolfe appeared not to notice. He was staring off into space as if unaware of his surroundings.

'Sorry about the misunderstanding over your boys. I sure got that all wrong. They was hanged already before you signed that there confession.' McCluskey shook his head. 'I never was much good with dates. It seems that confession got me into a mite of trouble. That smart-ass shyster is putting it about that I beat that confession outta you. I can't understand some people. I wouldn't hurt a fly.'

The man he was taunting did not seem to be listening. It eventually got to the big gaoler. He put his face close to the chained-up man.

'What does it take to rile you, Wolfe? I fool you with that there confession and you don't complain. You just sit there like a piece of shit. I knew them boys was dead when I got you to sign that confession. What'd think of that?'

The prisoner did not make any response.

McCluskey balled his fist and raised it as if he were about to strike the seated man. There was still no reaction from his charge. He hesitated then lowered his fist. Instead he bent till his face was inches from Zacchaeus Wolfe.

'I'm taking you to Clarksville, Wolfe. Charlie Greenalch and myself. Corporal Charlie Greenalch is one right mean bastard. He carries a meat-cleaver round with him. Twice he's been locked away for chopping bits off men he doesn't like. Each time he's been released. You know why? 'Cause he makes a soufflé for the colonel. Can you believe that? A goddamn soufflé! The colonel, he reckons he can't live without Corporal Greenalch's soufflé. So he sentences him to thirty days but releases him early to make this goddamn soufflé.'

The sergeant straightened up. His prisoner still did not show any reaction to the big man's presence.

'You're a dangerous man, Wolfe.' At this point the sergeant leant down and poked a blunt finger into Zacchaeus Wolfe's chest. As he spoke his finger jabbed again and again, digging hard into the material of the prisoner's uniform. 'So dangerous that when you make a break for it on the way to Clarksville, Charlie and I will have to kill you. You fought hard. I'll give you that much. Only Charlie was there with his cleaver or you might have overpowered us and got clean away. You see that's why I want Charlie with me. When we bring you in with bits hanging off they'll believe it was all Charlie's doing. He already has a reputation for flying off his meat cleaver handle.' Again he straightened and looked with some disgust at the prisoner. 'You know, you remind me of a pet dog I had once. I used to beat the hell outta that animal and it lay there and took it all. No matter what I did it never tried to bite me. It didn't even snarl. It just lay there and whimpered. I would tread on its paw till the blood oozed out between its pads and it would cry with the pain. I took a stick one day and even dug its eye out and still it wouldn't fight back. In the end I was so fed up with its cowardly nature I drowned it. Tied a rock around its scrawny neck and throwed it in the river.' The man shook his head in disgust. 'I guess I feel the same about you, Wolfe. You make me sick sitting there taking all this crap from me. You ain't a man at all – just a cowardly, mangy dog.'

He turned and walked out of the cell. As he slammed the cell door he did not see the man sitting on the bed raise his arms and look at the manacles on his wrists, nor did he hear the man as he spoke.

'A wolf, my friend, not a dog – a wolf.'

16

In the morning the big sergeant and the corporal with the fearful meat-cleaver reputation came for the prisoner.

'On your feet, you piece of scum.'

Corporal Greenalch was a tall, wiry man with a neat, goatee beard and dark, smouldering eyes.

Chains rattled as the prisoner stood upright. At all times he wore manacles on wrists and ankles. He had not been permitted to shave and a grey-tinged, tangled matt of hair obscured the lower half of his face. Anyone who had known Zacchaeus Wolfe prior to his arrest would have been shocked at his appearance. In fact very few would have recognized him now in the dishevelled garb of a jail-bird.

The corporal pushed the prisoner roughly out of the cell. McCluskey waited in the corridor, a sneer on his big beefy face. As the prisoner drew level he too punched him savagely so that he staggered forward.

It was like that all the way to the stables. The two men took great delight in harrying and hitting the prisoner. In spite of the chains on his ankles he did not fall. He stumbled from time to time but managed to keep on his feet. Three saddled cavalry mounts awaited them.

'Get up on that dun,' McCluskey ordered the manacled man.

Zacchaeus stood looking at the horse. 'I won't be able to sit astride with these chains on my legs,' he said at last.

McCluskey punched the prisoner. It was a hard blow to the side of the head. Zacchaeus saw it coming and rolled with the punch. He bounced against the side of the horse and it skittered nervously for a few paces.

'When I give you an order, you obey. You don't make difficulties. Now get on that horse.'

With that he lifted the smaller man and tossed him lightly like a sack of grain on to the back of the horse. The prisoner ended up draped across the saddle with head dangling one side and his feet on the other. Corporal Greenalch laughed out loud.

'Damn me, McCluskey, if you ain't as strong as a goddamn ox.'

McCluskey grinned back at his companion, then swung on to his own mount. The big sergeant took the reins of the dun and moved out to the gate with the corporal following. The sentries smartly saluted the mounted men. Once on the road the three rode abreast with Zacchaeus Wolfe in the middle. He was left dangling awkwardly across his mount.

'You comfortable there, Mr Wolfe, or would you like me to order a carriage for you?'

There was no response from the prisoner and they jogged on in silence for a while. Eventually Greenalch unhooked his canteen. He took a long swig from it and removing it from his mouth burped with satisfaction.

'You want some of this, McCluskey?'

'What the hell is it?'

'Some good old John Barleycorn.'

The big sergeant took the proffered canteen and smelt the contents. 'Damn me, if that don't smell good.' He drank deeply and handed the canteen back with a contented sigh. 'Ah, that sure wakes a man up in the morning.'

The canteen passed back and forth between the tall

corporal and the big sergeant. They grew animated and bright-eyed.

'When we gonna deal with this piece of shit we dragging along here?'

'Just as soon as we find a suitable place. We'll need to ride off the road a piece.'

The trail was winding through a densely wooded area. Here and there could be seen the devastation caused by heavy timber-harvesting. McCluskey turned off the trail and headed into one such clearing. Raw stumps of shaved-off trees stretched out like a scar on the land. They were well hidden from the road. Giving each other knowing looks the soldiers finished the contents of the canteen.

They dismounted and walked to the third horse across which their helpless prisoner was draped. Grabbing the manacled legs, McCluskey heaved upwards. Zacchaeus Wolfe tipped up head first on to the ground. His chained hands stretched out and hit the ground first. Neither of the soldiers noticed how the prisoner curled his body and rolled into the drop.

McCluskey slapped the horse on the rear and it shambled away. The prisoner lay on his back blinking and looking disoriented. The big sergeant bent down to grasp his victim. Zacchaeus Wolfe offered his manacled wrists to the sergeant. The big man grinned and reached for the chain running between the wrists. In one swift movement the prisoner brought his arms back and flung the chain up and over the sergeant's head. He rolled to one side, at the same time kicking the big man's legs from under him. The chain twisted neatly around the man's throat. With a swift, deft movement the sergeant was lying on top of his prisoner with the steel chain of the manacles biting into the flesh of his neck.

'Aaagh. . . .' His hands came up to grapple at the brutal links digging into his throat. It was a futile effort. Already the links were half-buried in the soft flesh and the sergeant's face was purpling as his air was cut off. He could not call out but could only make gasping, strangling noises as his prisoner lay underneath him using all the strength of his arms to garrotte his prey.

Corporal Greenalch could only gape as the tables were turned so abruptly on his companion. He took in the sergeant's purpling face and it was moments before he could take in the significance of the life-and-death struggle that was taking place before him.

'Goddamn, let him go, you bastard!' he yelled and flung himself at the struggling men.

Minutes of precious time were lost as he tried to pull the chain from his friend's neck. Cursing and screaming threats, he frantically searched for a gap to insert his fingers. No such gap was to be found. He struck at the prisoner's arms and hands and found he was striking solid bands of muscle with no give in their rigidity as their owner throttled the life from the big soldier who had tormented him when he was a helpless prisoner.

The sergeant's struggles were becoming feebler. His hands scrabbling at the chain embedded in his neck were covered in blood, as nails tore from sockets in his frantic struggle for life. The craggy face was a deep purple and the man's mouth was gaping wide. His tongue protruded like a piece of raw liver from bloody lips where he had bitten convulsively in his agony.

Corporal Greenalch rolled away from the struggling men. Scrambling to his feet he ran to his horse. His hands were trembling as he searched frantically in his saddlebags. When he'd found what he was searching for he turned around and ran back to his now weakly struggling friend. In his hand he carried the meat-cleaver – the instrument which, McCluskey had boasted, would end Zacchaeus Wolfe's life.

'Die, you bastard,' he screamed and swung a vicious blow at the man who was inexorably strangling the life from his friend.

Zacchaeus evaded the blow by pulling McCluskey into the path of the cleaver. If he had been able to, McCluskey would have screamed as the keen blade of the cleaver bit deep into his shoulder. As it was his eyes were already open as wide as they would go, as was his mouth, now encrusted with bloody foam.

It was Corporal Greenalch who screamed as he saw the result of his attack. He raised his weapon again searching for an opening. All the while this was going on the big sergeant was dying. His hands dropped from their frantic scrabbling at that unyielding chain now embedded in his neck and his feet ceased drumming on the earth. Again Corporal Greenalch screamed and then went berserk.

He raised the fearful blade and slashed wildly at the men on the ground unmindful of where it went or whom it injured.

Sparks bounced off the prisoner's chain as steel met steel. The man on the ground rolled frantically and tried to keep his victim between himself and the frenzied attack. Again and again the cleaver bit into the flesh of the big beefy sergeant.

The chain that Zacchaeus had used so effectively as a weapon now became a hindrance. It bound him inexorably to the dead and considerable weight of Sergeant McCluskey. Unable to free himself from his victim Zacchaeus Wolfe desperately wriggled and manoeuvred as the steel blade hammered down at him. The inevitable happened. It was his wrist that took the blow.

Zacchaeus almost screamed out as he felt the blade bite into flesh. He wrenched back from the sudden pain and astonishingly his arm came free from the manacle that, up till then, had bound him to the dead sergeant. For a

moment he stared at the bloody stump where before had
been a hand.

Pain and shock was one thing – survival was another
matter. Zacchaeus Wolfe was a survivor. He had survived in
the war because he had an animal instinct for survival. In
spite of the dreadful wound inflicted on him he went on
the attack.

Corporal Greenalch was raising his weapon for another
strike when out of the welter of bleeding and hacked flesh
a bloody stump erupted and hit him in the face. Blood
splattered into his eyes, blinding him. He stepped back to
clear his vision. Something hard and vicious cracked into
the side of his head. Again he stumbled back and again
that vicious and extremely painful thing cracked against
his head. Dazed and frightened he went back, but that
brutal attack never let up.

Through his pain and confusion he saw Zacchaeus
Wolfe advancing towards him as he retreated. The prisoner was flailing the loose end of his manacle at the corporal. On the end of the chain was the wrist-manacle – a
hoop of crude metal. It was this that the prisoner was using
to batter Corporal Greenalch. Under the vicious assault
the corporal went down. He cowered on the ground with
his arms wrapped around his head, trying to protect
himself from that rudimentary flail. It was fruitless. That
dreadful makeshift weapon slowly battered his hands into
useless lumps of bloodied flesh.

'Enough, enough!' he screamed, 'Please, I beg of you,
enough!'

Thankfully the terrible punishment stopped.

Breathing heavily, Zacchaeus Wolfe stepped back and
looked at his damaged arm. He blinked in surprise. The
hand was missing. Blood dripped from the stump unceas-
ingly. Turning from the cowering corporal Zacchaeus
looked around him. The cleaver lay where the corporal

had dropped it. With his good hand he picked up the bloodstained weapon and staggered over to the horses. In moments he had cut the harness straps. He dropped to his knees and, using his good hand and his teeth, he wrapped the leather tightly around his wrist and made an effective tourniquet. Blood ceased to flow from the arm. Only then did Zacchaeus slump to the ground. For long moments he stared round at the scene of the fight.

Sergeant McCluskey lay in a welter of blood and hacked flesh. His companion Corporal Greenalch was sitting with his knees drawn up to his chest. He was a gruesome sight with his head and face a mess of bloody lumps and cuts. He was staring at his useless, ruined hands held trembling before him.

17

Corporal Greenalch stared fearfully at the frightful man as he walked over to stand before him. The man was holding the corporal's meat-cleaver in his hand.

'Where's the key?'

The corporal stared uncomprehendingly at the man swaying before him. 'Key . . . what key. . . ?'

In reply Zacchaeus held up the cleaver and indicated the manacle dangling from his wrist. 'The key to these damned irons.'

'Sergeant McCluskey, he has the key.'

Zacchaeus went to the heap of mangled flesh that had been Sergeant McCluskey and searched the pockets. At last he found what he wanted. Grunting with the effort he bent down and fumbled the manacles on his ankles free. Then he took the key in his mouth and with some difficult manipulation managed to unlock his one remaining wrist-fetter. The effort seemed to tire him for he sat slumped for some time on a tree-stump.

Corporal Greenalch watched him fearfully. Eventually Zacchaeus stood and pushed the cleaver inside his belt. He picked up the discarded chains, walked to the blood-ied soldier and tossed them down before him.

'Put them on.'

The corporal held up his damaged hands. 'I can't.'

Zacchaeus regarded him critically for a moment. Then

he reached for the manacles and, squatting down, fumbled one-handed to attach the chains to his prisoner's ankles. It was only then that the corporal noticed the bloody stump. His eyes widened.

'Did I do that?'

Zacchaeus did not answer.

'You gonna kill me, Mr Wolfe? I'm sorry about your hand.'

The cold-eyed stare he received in reply did nothing to reassure him. Zacchaeus managed to fix one of the wrist-fetters onto his prisoner.

'Stand up.'

Fearfully the corporal stood and Zacchaeus dragged him towards one of the few trees still standing. Greenalch shuffled forward with his ankles shackled together.

'Put your hands above your head.'

When the corporal did so Zacchaeus flung the free end of the shackles over a low branch and again with some effort managed one-handed to fasten the manacle to the man's remaining wrist. Corporal Greenalch was now shackled hand and foot with the chain draped over the branch. It was possible he could free himself from the branch but only with a lot of effort and with his hands in the state they were there would be a lot of pain also.

Zacchaeus leant against the tree. His face was drained of colour and his dark, sunken eyes had retreated even further into their sockets.

'Tell me who ordered the killing.'

'Uh, you what?'

'I haven't much time, Corporal. Now if you want to live you'll answer my questions. If you answer my questions you might just live long enough to get those wounds attended to before gangrene sets in. Now, who ordered you to kill me?'

'It was a fella called Aaron. I only knew him through

McCluskey. McCluskey used to play cards with him. That's all I know, mister. Honest to God. I never wanted to come on this trip but McCluskey talked me into it.'

With some effort Zacchaeus levered his body from the tree against which he had been leaning. Slowly he walked to the horses.

'What you gonna do to me?'

There was no answer and Corporal Greenalch watched apprehensively as the wounded man worked awkwardly at his tasks. He gathered the reins of the horses and tied them together. Then he went to the body of Greenalch's dead companion and retrieved his army revolver. Returning to the horses he took Sergeant McCluskey's canteen and placing it underneath his arm used his remaining hand to unscrew the cap. He took a long drink before replacing the canteen back on the saddle. Then he took a protracted look around the scene of violence before hauling himself up on to McCluskey's big mare.

'Where you going?' the dangling man called out querulously.

The mounted man urged the horses forward. All three horses started off.

'Where you going?' screamed Corporal Greenalch. 'What about me?'

There was no response. The horses plodded on back towards the trail, leaving the clearing behind.

'You can't leave me here! How am I to get loose?'

Zacchaeus slumped in the saddle, his arm a throbbing mess of fire and pain. The horses plodded steadily forward. He was in no hurry. He would have liked to stay in the clearing and rest but the screaming man hanging from the tree-branch would have disturbed him.

The horses plodded along with steady rhythm. The screams faded into the distance. There was nothing to do but hold on to consciousness. He knew he must not fall asleep. Loss of blood caused sleepiness. He had seen it so many times. Fighting the drowsiness he tried to think ahead.

There were things he had to do. But first he must recover from his terrible wound. A one-handed man would be at a disadvantage in the world he now inhabited. It was a world filled with enemies who killed with callous disregard. His family had been slaughtered by these people – Quinton, Marty and Murdock. He tried to recall the last time he had seen them all together.

It was the day Barnabas had declared his love for Lavinia. Their mirth on that occasion was the result of youthful mischievousness. It had been occasioned to disconcert Barnabas and embarrass their sister. Now all were dead. Young lives snuffed out. He wondered what had happened to Lucius and to Lavinia. Their grief would be as heartfelt as was his own.

On he travelled with only these black and dire thoughts for his comfort. And pain – the pain of a missing limb was not so severe as the pain for the loss of his brother's children.

He knew intimately the country he was travelling in. Using little-known trails he guided his mounts along, always heading in the same direction.

He had plenty of time. No one would discover Corporal Greenalch for days, if he ever were discovered. Judging by the state of his damaged hands he would not be able to free himself from his constraints.

Knowing the army as he did it would be days before someone missed the men who were escorting the prisoner. It would be days more before a search-party would be sent out. Weeks might elapse before any action took place. By then he would be well hidden. But first he had to have help. There was only one place where he could get that help and he must stay awake and stay on top of his horse till he got there.

18

'What we gonna do with you, boy, now your old master is away in prison. We don't know when we gonna see him again.'

As Seth talked he threw chunks of raw meat into the cage. The half-grown wolf cub stared at him with smoky eyes. The animal's teeth were bared in a snarl and a low trembling growl vibrated from deep within its chest.

Seth had helped Zacchaeus build the cage. They had constructed it from the split logs they had been using in rebuilding the wrecked fencing around the property. It was roomy so that Zacchaeus could sit inside with the wolf in his efforts to tame it. He would sit quietly and toss little titbits of food to the young wolf.

No one else would be bothered with it. Seth knew Zacchaeus only troubled himself with the animal because it had been a present from his nephews. The rancher worshipped the boys and would have in no way offended them by neglecting the gift they had presented to him even if it had been in the nature of a joke.

The black cowhand cocked his head and listened as he heard horses on the road. He arose and walked round to the front of the house. Four horsemen jogged up the road before turning into the yard. They dismounted and walked towards the house, ignoring Seth.

'Howdy, what can I do for you gents?'

The men stopped walking and turned slowly to face the cowhand. Seth eyed them uneasily. The men gave off an aura of menace. He could see they were all dressed in the same outfits – long leather coats reaching to the heels of their boots, derby hats and guns strapped around the waist. Their faces were lean and their eyes were cold and unfriendly. Without warning one of the foursome stepped forward and in a smooth, swift movement drew his revolver and brought it down with considerable force on top of Seth's head. The cowhand collapsed and sprawled on the ground.

'Nobody asked you to speak, you piece of trash. Maybe you'll be a bit more respectful when in the presence of your betters.'

The stranger was pointing the gun at the cowhand. Seth stared up in a daze at the man. He felt a tickling sensation on his forehead and something wet dripped down his face. The cowhand said nothing. He had met this sort of hostility before, so he dropped his eyes and stayed where he was.

His head was pounding and he wanted to raise his hand and massage the injury. Seconds ticked by as the men waited. Then, seeing Seth was not going to retaliate, the man holstered his weapon and the four turned and continued on their walk to the front door. The injured cowhand stared after the men. A fear was on him as he watched them march up to the front door and enter without knocking.

There were only two people in the house and both were female. One was Seth's wife Angelina and the other was Lavinia. Seth pushed himself to his feet, fighting the waves of dizziness. He staggered round to the back of the house and went quietly into the kitchen. His mission was to warn Angelina not to rile the strangers. He was too late. He could hear her voice berating someone. Then her yells

93

were cut off abruptly.

Seth cursed and peered into the hallway. There was some sort of disturbance on the stairway.

'There's no one here only Miss Lavinia and she's hurt bad. You can't go up there.'

Seth tiptoed across the hallway. Under the stairs in a cupboard were stored the hunting-rifles and small arms. Seth chose the shotgun and loaded both barrels. He picked a revolver and pushed that into his waistband. Seth was not a gunman but he was the only man in the house and he felt it his duty to protect the household. He stepped out into the hall, the shotgun pointed towards the stairs.

Angelina was slowly reversing up the staircase. The men in the duster coats were advancing after her. They saw the widening of her eyes as she spotted Seth. As one they swung round and in less than a heartbeat four revolvers were pointed at the cowboy. No one said anything. No order was given. Four guns exploded as one and a hail of lead swept the young cowhand from his feet. He had no time to fire his shotgun. He was dead as he hit the carpet and the shotgun fell beside him unfired.

In the silence that followed the shots Angelina screamed. One of the gunmen cursed and swung his revolver towards her.

'Shut up that damn caterwauling 'less you want to join that dead fella in the hall.'

Angelina sat abruptly on the step and stared with tragic eyes at her dead husband. 'You killed him,' she whimpered. 'You killed my Seth.' She lifted her apron, buried her face in the material and began to wail, rocking back and forth on the stairs.

'Leave her,' one of the men growled. 'Eldridge said there was only these black hands out here. We'll have a look around. See who this Lavinia person is she was on about.'

They filed past the grieving woman and continued their search.

'Here,' one of them called.

They crowded into the room and stared at the girl on the bed. She was lying motionless, her face carved in white marble. A bandage was wound about her neck beginning just under her chin and continuing down over the throat so that no flesh was visible.

'Jesus, she was a good-looking kid.'

'Is she dead?'

'Sure looks like it.'

The man who spoke bent over the girl.

'Eldridge never said nothing about her. He just said about the black cowhands. Never mentioned no dead girl.'

'Goddamn it, I think she's still breathing. What we gonna do?'

'Hell, I donno. We gotta clear everyone out. Let's have a word with that black bitch downstairs. We can pretend we gonna fire the house. We'll go and put the fear of hell into her. Hell, we shouldn't have killed that black fella. He would have helped get her outta here.'

They found Angelina kneeling by her husband's body cradling his head in her hands. She turned her grief-swollen face towards the men who had killed her man so callously.

'Why'd you have to kill him? He was a good man. He looked after the ranch for Mr Wolfe when he was away at the war. You nothing but murdering scum.'

'Hell, he had a gun and was gonna shoot us. We hadn't time to ask questions. In our game if you don't act fast you more'n likely get killed. Anyways, what's done can't be undone. What's wrong with the girl we found upstairs? She sure looks more dead than alive.'

'Miss Lavinia! Don't you go messing with Miss Lavinia!

She hurt real bad. Doctor Langdon he say she can't be moved.' As her concern for Lavinia grew Angelina rose to her feet.

'She'll have to be moved. Our orders are to clear the house and then set fire to everything.'

'You can't do that! This house belong Master Wolfe!'

'Not any more, sister. Our orders are to clear everyone out and set fire to it. The railroad is coming through here. Everything has to be cleared.

'Look, sister, we'll give you a break. What if we ride outta here and go back to town? We'll come back in the morning to fire the house. That'll give you time to move the girl out. You can take her into town. Someone'll take her in.'

The rest of the gang were clattering down the stairs.

'No one else in the house,' one of them announced.

'Right, fellas, have a look around outside in case there's someone else here. Eldridge mentioned a couple of cowhands. The other might be hiding out somewhere. I told the woman we'd give them a break and come back in the morning and do the burning. That girl in the bed upstairs gives me the creeps. I don't want to have to mess around with her. With a bit of luck they'll move out and give us no more bother. We can tell Eldridge we cleared the place.'

Angelina watched in despair as the men filed past her without a second glance at the dead man sprawled in the hall. She ran for the stairway and flew up the stairs afraid of what she would find in Lavinia's bedroom. It was with some relief she saw the girl undisturbed. Sitting by the injured girl she buried her face in her hands and wept bitter tears of anger and grief.

19

Up in the foothills Tobias heard the shots. He stared in the direction of the ranch house, then turned his mount around and began a slow and cautious descent towards the ominous sounds. When he came in sight of the house he stopped and watched. A group of four men spilled out of the house and into the yard. They divided up and began to search the barns and outhouses. Tobias removed the Winchester from his saddle bucket and rested it across his saddle horn.

It was only when he observed the men climb on their horses and ride away back in the direction of town that he nudged his pony into motion.

He left his mount on the road and came on to the house on foot. The front door was standing open. He listened and from inside he could hear a soft sobbing. Cautiously he pushed inside and stopped short as he tried to make sense of the shocking spectacle he was witnessing in the once peaceful household.

Slowly Tobias reached up and pushed his hat to the back of his head. He leaned against the doorway and stared, not really wanting to believe what his eyes were telling him.

Seth and he had arrived as two frightened boys at the Wolfe ranch. Old Master Wolfe and his wife had greeted them kindly and within a short time the boys had realized that they had arrived at a safe haven. Since then their loyalty and love of the Wolfe family had never been in any doubt.

The two young slaves had seen very little of the older Wolfe boy, Makepeace, for he was mostly away at college training to be a preacher. Zacchaeus, the younger son, on the other hand had always been around and was responsible for teaching the new slaves how to look after livestock and all the skills related to running a ranch. Now Tobias leaned hard against the fabric of the house and tears came to his eyes as he looked at the blood-soaked body of his boyhood friend.

Kneeling by his side, Seth's wife Angelina was sobbing so hard she did not notice the cowhand enter. Still carrying his rifle he stepped inside, trying hard to force down his grief. Slowly he crouched by his friend and reached out a hand to stroke his hair. It was only then that Angelina saw him.

'Oh, Tobias, they shot him down. My Seth is no more. What am I gonna do?'

He shifted round and placed an arm around her.

'I sure dunno, Angelina. This family sure got some sorta curse on it. But I sure never thought it would reach out and touch us too.'

He rose and at the same time gently lifted up the weeping woman with him. 'Come in the kitchen and make me some coffee. You can tell me what happened.'

With his arm still around her shoulders Tobias led the weeping woman towards the kitchen. While she put water on the stove he had a sudden dreadful thought.

'What about Miss Lavinia? Did they find her?'

'Poor Miss Lavinia, thank the Lord they didn't interfere with her. Tobias, they say we gotta vacate the house. Theys coming back in the morning to set fire to everything. The railroad wants the land or something. Oh, Tobias, what we gonna do?'

Tobias sat absorbing this information. He was sunk in his thoughts so deeply Angelina had to nudge him to show him the steaming mug of coffee she had placed in front of him. When at last he looked up at her his eyes were stricken with some dire foreboding.

'This family is cursed. Don't you see, Angelina – a witch has hexed them for something one of them done. First Master Quinton is killed. Then Master Zacchaeus is arrested. While he in prison Master Barnabas, what Miss Lavinia is to marry, is killed. Master Marty and Master Murdock is hanged for the murder what I guess they did not do. And Miss Lavinia is taken and abused and left for dead and her life is only hanging on by a thread. Now Seth lies dead out there in the hall.'

He picked up his mug of coffee and sat sipping it, staring off into some frightful future.

'What we to do, Tobias? Will the curse take us too?'

'We the only ones left – you and me and Miss Lavinia?'

For a moment neither spoke.

'What about Reverend Makepeace?' Angelina asked in a hushed voice.

'Reverend Makepeace he a preacher, maybe he can keep the curse away from hisself. We gotta protect ourselves and Miss Lavinia. You say them fellas coming back in the morning to fire the place?'

Angelina nodded.

'There's only one place we can go. We gotta seek out Momma Gabrielle – ask for her protection.'

Angelina's eyes widened. 'Momma Gabrielle – you don't believe all that voodoo stuff, Tobias?'

'I dunno, Angelina, but what else is there?'

'And Miss Lavinia, what about her?'

'We gotta take her with us. If she left behind she is in great danger. The fellas what attacked her left her for dead and she would have been, only I found her. If they find out she still alive and can identify them then they'll come to finish her off. Can't you see, we ain't got no option. We gotta pack up now and get away from this place.'

'What about my Seth, Tobias?'

Tobias looked soberly at his friend's widow. 'We'll take Seth with us. We'll give him a decent burial. I don't know about Momma Gabrielle and her voodoo magic but it's all we got now. There's no one else to help us with Master Zacchaeus in prison and Reverend Makepeace out of his mind with grief.'

They rolled the body of Seth in the carpet where he had bled away his life and carried it out to the farm wagon. Tobias and Angelina lifted the mattress from the bed on which the pale form of Lavina was lying and carried her downstairs and placed the whole thing in the wagon alongside the body of Seth.

'Collect as much food as you can to take with us,' Tobias instructed Angelina. 'Leave nothing of value for them vultures. I'll collect the rifles and ammunition and see if there is any money lying around and small valuables we can perhaps sell. Miss Lavinia will need medicines and Momma Gabrielle don't work for nothing. I'll round up what horses I can find and take them as well. Maybe we can sell them.'

In a very short time the laden wagon lurched from the Wolfe ranch. Tobias drove while inside the wagon Angelina watched over her charges, one of whom was dead and the other near to death.

The young wolf waited patiently. When all was quiet it began to feed. The hunks of meat Seth had left were gobbled down rapidly. Then it began the ceaseless pacing up and down the cage. Back and forth it went restlessly, seeking some escape from the cage.

20

'Have you bought the Wolfe ranch yet, Samuel?'

'Sure, Pinkertons came in and told me they cleared the place. I got one of my clerks handling the paperwork.'

'I been thinking about that ranch, Samuel, it has a fine big house and there is plenty of land goes with it. What if we went back to the original route surveyed by your poor murdered brother and I was to move into the house.'

Samuel lent back in his chair and gazed at Tamara. He could not help thinking how stunning she looked. Her red hair hung down in long soft waves. On one side the hair fell forward and covered that half of her face and she had an endearing habit of flicking her head to tease the wayward strands out of her line of vision. Large hazel eyes gazed steadily back at him. Even though he was busy with paperwork he had an almost irresistible desire to stand and kiss her. Red full lips that glistened slightly with some cosmetic almost invited him to do just that.

'You know, Tamara, you are utterly gorgeous.'

She was five years his senior and he had never met any woman who affected him as she did.

'Come and sit on my knee and tell me again what you have in mind,' he invited.

There was faint seductive smile on her lips as she complied. He inhaled her scent and buried his face in her luxuriant red hair.

'What I have in mind is not for a lady to express in actual words,' she murmured in his receptive ear.

He grinned and kissed her cheek. 'I mean about the house, silly woman. And I have exactly the same thing in mind.'

She curled her arms around his neck and pouted seductively. 'This town house is not what I'm used to. I have no room to express myself. I wondered if the Wolfe residence would be more in keeping with my station in life. After all, we are not married and yet we're living in the same house. I don't want people to gossip about me.'

'Darling, I thought that was all taken care of with your family living under the same roof.'

'What did you pay for the Wolfe place?'

He grinned at her. 'Five hundred dollars.'

Her eyes opened wide at this revelation. 'Five hundred for the whole estate! My, my, you certainly got a bargain there. What about the stock and all?'

'That's extra cream on the cake. Officially stock was not included in the sale. We bought just the land. However, as the owner was in prison . . .' he shrugged, 'I thought I might just do a little bit of inventive paperwork and take possession of the lot.'

'Samuel, you're a financial wizard. No wonder you are a rich man.'

'Yeah, and I intend to become a lot richer. That land is worth a hell of a lot more than five hundred as you can well guess.'

He sat thinking for a short spell and Tamara was moved to ask, 'What's going on in that fevered brain of yours?'

'You've given me an idea. As director of South West Railroad I'm not strictly supposed to own land that could be used by the company. What if I carried through the sale of the Wolfe place in your name?

'I've been studying the reports that Barnabas filed

before those people killed him. He routed the railroad around the back of those hills that border on the Wolfe ranch. I think he was trying to save the ranch for his girl-friend and her family. Barnabas was to marry her – that Lavinia one – the daughter of the preacher. Maybe Barnabas thought the land might become more valuable if the railroad decided to come through the ranch instead of circumscribing it as in his original survey. Once married to Lavinia he would be in a position to get a slice of the wealth generated by the sale at an inflated price to the rail-road. Perhaps Barnabas was not as naïve as I originally thought.' He slid his hands up under Tamara's armpits. 'How would you like to be a landowner?'

'I would love it. However, I have not the money to buy that place even at the knockdown price of five hundred.'

He pulled her against him and pushed his face into her breasts.

'Don't you worry your pretty head about such mundane matters as money to buy property. I have sufficient for us both.' He leaned back and regarded her. 'We buy the Wolfe ranch in your name for five hundred dollars and we carry out the original scheme envisaged by Barnabas. No suspicion will fall on me, as the deed will be in your name. When the time is ripe we sell it to the railroad for a good deal more than we paid for it. I feel that it would be a fitting memorial to my dear brother. At least something of his lives on in this venture.'

'Samuel, you are a financial wizard. I only wish that dreadful man Zacchaeus Wolfe had lived to learn of how we disposed of his family home.'

Samuel frowned at her. 'What do you mean, had lived to learn of this? I heard nothing of his death. He was to be transferred to Clarksville to be tried by the military there. That damn slick lawyer got him that reprieve anyway, though I have a feeling he's going to work some chicanery to save the fella's bacon.'

'I . . . I mean that he should have been here to see the people he hated move into his home. But you're right; he might just escape justice. I wish my boys had managed to kill him that day they accidentally shot his nephew. Maybe then your Barnabas would be alive now.'

Samuel sighed. 'Well, let's forget all that. The past is behind us. We can't bring back the dead. Maybe they'll give him a long prison sentence. The whole family is bad. Lucius Wolfe has been sending me threats. He reckons he's going to exact revenge for the hanging of his brothers. For Christ's sake, what the hell does he expect? They murdered Barnabas – did they think I'd turn the other cheek? I ain't no preacher like his pa. Though maybe the Reverend Wolfe ain't so holy as he tries to make out. He sure raised a brood of hellhounds.'

'So when can I move out there?'

'You seem a mite anxious to get away from me,' he teased her.

She planted her lips against his and the kiss was long and lingering. When finally they broke apart she stroked his face. 'Do you think I can bear being away from you? You are going to be a frequent visitor. I was thinking of renaming the house. I want to call it Wolfsden.'

'Wolfsden!'

She giggled. 'It's my little joke. It really means Wolfe's Den.'

21

Zacchaeus Wolfe drifted in and out of delirium. His one remaining hand became a claw as he hung on to the reins of his mount. The animal plodded along placidly with the two captured mounts trailing behind. From time to time his nephews appeared and helped to guide him.

Quinton had on a bloody nightshirt. A large hole was discernible in his chest.

'I'm sorry, Quinton, I'm sorry you were shot.'

'It hurts, Uncle Zac, it hurts real bad. Am I gonna die?'

'I dunno, I'll do what I can for you. Tobias went for the doctor. He'll patch you up.'

His place was taken by Marty. A noose was draped round Marty's neck with the loose end dangling to the ground. From time to time Marty would tread on the loose end and stumble. His head would flop around on his neck. When he spoke his voice was hoarse and distorted.

'Uncle Zac, why didn't you come for us? We hung around waiting for you.'

'I . . . I . . . couldn't, Marty . . . I was in prison. They wouldn't let me out.'

'They hanged us!' It was Murdock screaming at him. 'They hanged us!'

Zacchaeus woke with a start and the bird screamed at him for riding beneath its tree.

'They hanged us!' the bird screamed and Zacchaeus shuddered.

'Leave me alone. I confessed my guilt. Sergeant McCluskey was too late. He got the dates mixed up.'

And Murdock's face changed again and the big sergeant grinned up at him as they ambled along.

'Aaron told me to kill you. He said your death was long overdue. Corporal Greenalch wants his cleaver back. He says he can't stand the pain of his hands any more. He wants to chop them off. Will you give it him back?'

'Yes,' mumbled Zacchaeus.

He searched frantically but did not know what he was looking for.

The horses clattered into the yard and Zacchaeus realized he was home. There were lights on in the house and he fell out of the saddle. For a long time he lay on his back in the dirt of the yard. Tears were in his eyes as he looked up into the star-studded sky.

'Lucius will help me – and Lavinia. Then I will have to go far away. I must be long gone from here when they come looking for me. But first I must have my hand fixed up. Lucius and Lavinia will help. All that's left of my family.' The tears flowed unheeded down his dirty face into his dishevelled, filthy beard.

After a few attempts he rolled on to his front and with great effort climbed to his feet. His feet stumbled as he mounted to the front door. He managed to open it and almost fell inside. As he lurched down the hall he heard voices in the living-room. A woman was laughing and he heard the rumble of a man's voice.

'Lavinia,' he whispered and pushed open the door.

The couple on the couch did not notice the dirty figure in the doorway. The woman was sitting with her arms around the man – the front of her dress unbuttoned. On her face was an ecstatic look and she moaned with obvious pleasure. The swarthy man beside the woman was smiling at her, showing off a mouthful of gold teeth.

'Lavinia . . .' whispered Zacchaeus, 'what are you doing. . . ?'

The man jerked his head and saw the filthy thing in the doorway. Blood and gore smeared the creature's face and hair. Most of it had splashed on to Zacchaeus when Corporal Greenalch had hacked at his friend with his meat-cleaver. In spite of his preoccupation with the woman the gunman's reaction was instantaneous. With a swift movement he reached beneath the low couch and came up with a pistol. The woman, sensing his movement, opened her eyes and, seeing the pointing gun, followed it and saw Zacchaeus. She screamed and made an attempt to cover herself. She stared in horror at the filthy apparition.

Aaron held his fire as he perceived there seemed to be no immediate threat.

'What the hell you mean, old man, barging in here?'

The red-haired woman shuffled off her lover and sank on to the seat, clutching her dress around her. Her face was shocked and her eyes were staring in horror at the foul creature that had so abruptly interrupted her pleasure.

By now Aaron was sitting up and, unlike the woman, making no attempt to cover his state of undress.

'Who are you, old man? What you looking for?'

'Lavinia, you can't do that with your brother. What would your father say? I hope he never finds out. This is gross . . . this is gross. . . .'

'You crazy old pervert!' the woman screamed. 'Kill him, Aaron. Shoot the filthy creature!'

'Sure, honey, I'll shoot him, but not in here, not in our new house. He'll bleed all over the carpet.'

'Lavinia . . . you're not Lavinia.' Zacchaeus stared hard at the couple in the room. He was finding it hard to separate reality from delusion. And then the back of his head exploded and he pitched forward into the room. He was replaced in the doorway by the grinning face of Demetrius.

Slowly the grin faded as he stared at his mother in her disarrayed clothing. He glanced at Aaron and his face took on a bewildered expression.

'Ma, what's going on? Why are you and Aaron like this?'

His brother poked his head over his shoulder and he too stared with some surprise at Aaron's state of undress.

'What's going on, Ma?'

'It's not what you think, boys. It's just that Aaron had a disjointed back and I was trying to massage some comfort back into it.'

The boys ignored the unconscious figure of Zacchaeus lying inside the room. Aaron was smiling at the boys, his golden teeth glittering bizarrely against the swarthiness of his skin.

'Come on, boys, you know what goes on. Your ma and I go back a long way.'

'Wha . . . what about Eldridge. . . ? He ain't gonna take kindly to playing second fiddle.'

Again the golden-toothed gunman man smiled at the boys. 'What Eldridge don't know won't hurt him. Your ma needs a real man, not some pumped-up little clerk like Eldridge.' Aaron turned and looked at Tamara who was hastily trying to button up her dress. She glared at Aaron but he was enjoying this moment of arrogance and ignored her frowning disapproval. 'I surely ain't gonna tell him and I wouldn't advise you to go blabbing off your mouth to him. Now, if you're finished gawking at your ma and me you could do us a favour and drag that piece of filth outside.'

The brothers looked uncertainly at each other, then fixed their eyes on the prone figure lying motionless on the carpet.

'What'll we do with him?'

Aaron's grin grew even broader. He shrugged his shoulders and turned his back on the brothers. 'I'm sure you boys will think of something amusing.'

They bent and taking a leg each began to drag Zacchaeus

from the room. There was a dirty smear on the carpet to mark his passage. He was pulled along the hall and out of doors, his head bumping down the steps. In the yard the brothers paused and looked at the lifeless figure.

'Where the hell did he come from, I wonder?'

'My guess he's just a saddle bum. Them's mighty fine horses he brung along. Must'a stole them.'

'Hey, he's gotta gun.' Demetrius bent and removed the revolver from the waistband of the unconscious figure. He tossed the weapon on to the porch. It made a dull thud as it landed on the boards. 'Hell, I got me an idea.' He turned his gaze on his brother. 'The wolf!'

'What about the wolf?'

The brothers had discovered the caged wolf and had spent a pleasant hour tormenting the beast.

'How's about we put this old tramp in with the wolf? It'll tear him to pieces.'

Kieran began to dance around the unconscious man on the ground. 'Hellfire and damnation, Demetrius, that's brilliant.' Suddenly he stopped and gazed soberly at his brother. 'What about Ma and Aaron? Samuel is our ticket on the gravy-gain. If he finds out about them two it could jeopardize our easy life.'

Demetrius sobered also. 'Damn Aaron, it weren't right for him to stand there like that in front of Ma.' He kicked at the man on the ground. 'Maybe it's time Aaron met with a little accident. We could easily take him between us.'

The brothers eyed each other for a moment.

'Hell, let's take this bum to feed the wolf.'

Each took an ankle and dragged the unconscious man around the back of the house.

The wolf growled low in its throat when it caught the scent of its tormentors. Slowly it reversed to the furthest corner of the cage.

'Wolfie, look, we brought you your supper. Nice ripe

old man for you to eat. You don't mind a bit of dirt on your food, now do you?'

Giggling insanely the brothers dragged their bundle up to the cage door. Grunting with the effort they shoved the lifeless figure inside the enclosure. While they worked the wolf growled ceaselessly, its teeth exposed and ears drawn back. Hastily they shut the door of the cage and stepped back to watch what would happen. They fully expected the wolf to pounce upon the somnolent figure they had delivered to it. The animal made no attempt to approach the bundle of dirty humanity in the cage. It never took its baleful eyes from the two boys and never stopped that low rumbling deep in its chest.

'Goddamn thing, why ain't it eating that old bastard?'

Kieren started giggling. 'Maybe he's too ripe even for the wolf.'

'Let's drive it down the cage.'

They retrieved the poles they had used previously to torment the wolf and began to poke at it through the bars. The snarling grew in volume as the wolf reversed away from the prodding. It leapt and twisted in attempts to escape, snarling and biting at the poles. With all their efforts the boys could not get the wolf interested in the old saddle tramp they had deposited in the cage. At last, tiring of the game, they desisted and threw down their poles in disgust.

'Hell, that wolf is sure one ornery beast,' Demetrius said disgustedly.

'Maybe it just ain't hungry. Hell, we'll just leave it there. When it gets hungry it'll start eating the old bum. When we hear him scream we'll come out and watch. Let's get us a drink.'

They began to spar with each other, then broke apart and ran to the house shrieking and yodelling. In exuberant high spirits they crashed into the house. The door slammed behind them and the yard fell silent.

22

Snakebite Junction was a huddle of shacks that had grown up beside the Snake River. The main reason for its existence was the ford that provided easy crossing for horses and wagons.

Tobias urged his team of horses into the river. The water was fast-flowing at this point, having descended from the low-lying hills, but the pebbly river floor provided a firm and safe bottom for vehicles.

It had been a fraught journey as the wagon had lumbered along pitted roads. Tobias had tried to avoid the worst potholes on the roads in order to avoid jolting his fragile passenger. Now they were almost at their destination: He was sweating by the time the wagon lurched up the far bank and the track levelled out to enter the town.

They had arrived early in the afternoon. People came outdoors to stare at the new arrivals. Most of the faces watching the wagon were black. Tobias was aware of the town's reputation as a refuge for runaway slaves during the Civil War. He wondered how they would react if they knew he carried in the back of his wagon an injured white girl.

He examined the buildings as the horse team plodded along. A blacksmith's workshop was one of the first places they came to, then a restaurant, a cantina, livery stables, then goods-stores and offices. Tobias nodded to the huge black man standing in the doorway of the smithy. The man

111

smiled and nodded back. Inevitably the children appeared and wandered curiously alongside the wagon.

'Where you from, mister?'

'What you got in the wagon?'

Tobias ignored the questions and contented himself with a shrug and a wave of his hand. This did not satisfy the youngsters and they danced along beside the wagon chanting the questions over and over again. He pulled up outside the hotel and stared doubtfully at the dilapidated building. A sign announcing the Snake Bend Luxury Hotel hung crookedly from a beam.

'If this is luxury I sure wouldn't like to see the state of the flophouse,' he muttered under his breath. He turned and gazed into the interior of the wagon. 'How you-all doing there, Angelina?'

The distraught face of the young woman appeared beside him. 'I never been so scared in my life, I felt every bump and pothole we went over. My heart is sore from watching over my poor Seth and Miss Lavinia.'

Tobias reached out and placed his hand on her shoulder. 'Well, we've arrived. Wait here while I go in the hotel and enquire about rooms. It don't look much but I can't see no other accommodation.'

Wearily he climbed down and went inside.

A woman rose from a chair by the window and nodded to him. Tobias could not help staring at her. She was tall and willowy and very black. Her hair was gathered up on her head, exposing delicate shell-like ears from which dangled large gold earrings. She had a slim straight nose and high cheekbones. Her eyes were large and liquid with murky, deep-brown pupils. Tobias could not help staring for he had never seen anyone more beautiful.

'Can I help you?' she said in a melodious and richly vibrant voice.

'I ... I ... rooms ... we need somewhere to stay,'

Tobias stammered, overawed by the magnificent female.

The woman walked to a desk in one corner. 'A room for you and your wife, how many nights?'

'She . . . she's not my wife . . . there's two of them. I need a room for myself and a room for two females. One is very ill.'

'What is the matter with her?'

'She was attacked and badly hurt. I'm not sure she will survive.'

'Is there someone chasing you?'

Tobias shook his head. 'No, we were made homeless and decided to come here.'

She regarded him for a few moments, her lustrous eyes probing him as if assessing his truthfulness. 'Fifty cents a night per room with food extra.'

'That sounds mighty fine to me. The sick woman can't eat for now.'

'Do you need any help?'

He hesitated. 'We carried her on to the wagon on a mattress. I would appreciate some help getting her up to her room.'

The woman turned her head slightly. 'Denzil,' she called.

A young black man appeared from out back at her summons.

'Denzil will help you.'

As they carried the mattress inside the hotel the woman walked over and stared down at the pale, still figure of Lavinia. She placed her hand on the girl's forehead and held it there for a moment before turning her gaze on Tobias. 'You have witnessed much trouble, my friend. If you want I can try to help her. If you agree I will have her taken to my room.'

Tobias swallowed hard. 'Pardon me, ma'am, but I brought her here to seek the help of Momma Gabrielle.'

A faint smile touched her lips. 'Lucky for you, then, I am Momma Gabrielle.'

Denzil saw to his wants and when he had fed him took him down to the blacksmith to arrange the funeral for Seth.

'Tomorrow – tomorrow you can bury your friend.'

Tobias did not see any of the women until the next day when they emerged from the sick-room to attend the funeral of Seth.

Angelina gave him a wan smile when she saw him but did not speak. The hearse was a two-wheeled open cart drawn by an ancient mule – the coffin, a, pine box decorated with symbols and writing burned on with a hot poker. Momma Gabrielle conducted the burial-service.

Holding her arms wide and with closed eyes she prayed over the grave. At this stage Angelina broke down and Tobias placed his arm around her shoulders. He wanted to weep himself, for Seth and he had been friends for most of their lives. Back at the hotel he quizzed the women about Lavinia.

'You can come in and see her now, Tobias,' Momma Gabriel invited.

The sweet smell of burning incense sticks greeted him as he entered the darkened room. Dozens of candles positioned on shelves and furniture and even on the floor flickered and guttered, giving the room a shrine-like atmosphere. A bed was pushed against one wall and he could see the still form of Lavinia. Timorously he approached the bed and looked down at the injured girl. His heart leapt into his throat as she opened her eyes and looked up at him.

'You say a curse is on the family.'

Tobias nodded. Angelina was sitting by the bed holding Lavinia's hand. Tobias and Momma Gabrielle were standing at the foot of the bed while Tobias related to her the

114

tragic events of the past weeks.

'That's why I come to you. Can you lift the curse?'

The woman turned her luminous eyes on him. 'You say the men threatened to set fire to the house?'

Tobias nodded. 'That's why we fled. We had nowhere else to go.'

'I want you to go back there to the place where all these people lived. You will take with you a small sack, which I will bless and you will fill it with dirt from the front yard of this house. They will all have tramped across the yard and some imprint of their passing will be retained. Bring this to me and if it is within my power I will see to the lifting of the curse on this family.'

23

His mother was washing his face. She was using a rough flannel and with patient strokes worked steadily. He lay quietly allowing her gentle attention to soothe him. But nothing could stop the pain from coming to the surface. His whole arm was a hot, throbbing ache of agony and he felt as if his head was splitting in half. He moaned and forced his eyes open and stared into the eyes of the devil.

The devil had the face of an animal. He could feel its hot breath on his face as it licked at him with a long, moist tongue. He let his eyes travel along the animal's shape and figured it was lying alongside him. It reminded him of a wolf and he wondered at that.

'Are you my personal demon?' he croaked.

The wolf stopped licking and sat up on its haunches and regarded him soberly. Slowly he pulled himself upright and stared around him. He was in a cage of some kind.

'So this is hell,' he muttered. 'Brother Makepeace was right after all.'

Then the events of the last few days came flooding back and he realized with a sudden burst of lucidity where he was. He leaned against the bars of the cage and began to figure out how he had come to be in the cage with his pet wolf. The wolf sat a few feet away watching him.

'I realize now it was wrong to put you in this cage, Mr

Wolf. I've been in a cage this past while myself and it wasn't pleasant, to say the least.'

A wave of nausea swept over him and he leaned his head against the bars of the cage. Soberly he regarded his missing hand.

'At least you still got all your limbs, Mr Wolf. All we have in common is our loss of liberty.'

He took stock of his situation and began to feel around his person for the weapons he remembered holding. The Army Colt he had taken from Sergeant McCluskey was missing. Something hard and flat was pressing into his groin. With a bit of wriggling he managed to retrieve the meat-cleaver that had been Corporal Greenalch's preferred weapon. Having constructed the cage he knew instinctively the manner of his escape.

The hinges of the cage door were made from sturdy leather strips. Lifting the gate and dragging it achieved access. With painful and slow effort he moved to the end of the cage and began to attack the leather hinges with the cleaver. The material was thick and tough and Zacchaeus Wolfe was weak from loss of blood and the trauma of a hacked-away limb. He had to rest often.

The wolf settled down to watch.

Tobias cantered along on the look-out for other riders. He went across country and avoided the main trails. After all that had happened to the Wolfe family and his friend Seth he was taking no chances on running into trouble. For that reason also he had timed his trip so as to arrive at night.

As he neared the ranch he expected to encounter the rank stink of a burnt-out building. He was puzzled by the lack of such evidence that the house had gone up in flames. Only when he came in sight of the house did he realize the railroad toughs had not carried out their threat. He sat his pony, observing the ranch.

In the darkness of the night he could see lights in some of the windows. He decided to leave his pony and continue on foot. The sack he was to retrieve the dirt in was stuffed into his belt.

Cautiously he approached and crouched down by the perimeter fence to watch for signs of activity. The house seemed quiet and after some ten minutes he crept into the yard and, making sure no one was about, he knelt down and began to dig, using his knife. It was only hard-packed earth he was excavating and it did not take him long to fill the small sack. Carrying this in one hand he sheathed his knife. Curious as to what was going on he decided to chance a look in at the windows.

A man and woman were sitting together on the divan. The woman had her arms around the man and was nuzzling at his neck. It took Tobias a moment or two to figure out their identity.

'It's that gunslinger and the woman who was with the people what killed Quinton that day,' he muttered. He wondered what twist of fortune had put them in possession of the Wolfe ranch house.

A slight sound from behind alerted him and instinctively he whirled, swinging the sack of dirt. He saw the glitter of a blade and his improvised weapon deflected the down swing. He flung himself at his assailant and they both went down.

As he grappled with the attacker neither made a sound. The only noise was the grunting of men straining to kill each other. Frantically Tobias gripped the hand holding the blade. His other hand he wrapped round the man's throat. He could feel the wiry strength of his opponent. Then he was momentarily blinded as a head crashed into the bridge of his nose.

'Goddamn it,' he grunted, trying desperately to hold

on to his attacker. His vision cleared and he saw the man he was fighting was a grimy wretch of a fellow. The man's teeth were exposed in a grimace of effort as he tried to disable Tobias. His grip on the man's throat was dislodged as a forearm was smashed against his already suffering nose. Frantically he grappled for the man's free arm and managed to fend off any more blows. At that moment he heard a door open. He froze and to his relief his opponent went still also. It occurred to him neither of them wished to be discovered.

'What the hell's going on out there?'

A man was standing outlined against the lighted doorway. He held a pistol in his hand. Tobias realized it was the gunman he had seen through the window with the woman. It was disconcerting to lie in close embrace with a man who had been trying to kill him. A shape darted across the yard and the gunman fired instinctively at the fleeting movement.

'Aaron, what is it?' a woman's voice called.

'I'm not sure, I could have swore it was a wolf or a dog or something. Goddamn can't see a thing out here.'

'Oh, come on inside. It's cold with that door open.'

'Yeah, yeah, yeah, I'm coming.'

The door closed and Tobias turned his attention back to his present predicament. 'Who are you, fella? It seems to me we both on the same side.'

The man lying beneath Tobias grunted. 'Tobias, is that you?'

'Hell, you know me but who are you?'

He could feel the man relax. 'Tobias, it's me, Zacchaeus Wolfe. Let's get away from here. We can talk later.'

Before they reached the horse Tobias had left tethered away from the house Zacchaeus sagged on to the dirt.

'Go on without me, Tobias. I don't think I can make it.'

'I can't leave you here, Mr Zacchaeus.'

119

There was no answer. Tobias hunkered down and with some effort managed to lift Zacchaeus on to his shoulder. He grunted with the effort, surprised at how heavy the man was, remembering the previous occasion when he had carried another injured member of the Wolfe family.

With Zacchaeus slung across the front of his mount Tobias rode away from the Wolfe ranch. He wasn't sure if the burden his horse carried was alive or dead.

24

'Angelina, is that you?'

'Yes, Mr Wolfe, you take it easy now. I got some broth for you. Can you sit up for it or do you want me to spoon it you?'

Zacchaeus had woken in an unfamiliar room to find Angelina dabbing his face with a cool, moistened cloth.

'Where am I? This ain't the ranch.'

'Mr Wolfe, I ain't telling you nothing unless you sit up and take this here broth.'

He grimaced but did as she ordered and prised himself upright. He looked with some surprise at his neatly bandaged stump. Angelina noted his interest.

'Mr Wolfe, that was a terrible thing, you losing your hand like that.'

His arm ached but not as badly as he remembered. 'You sure did a good job on this, Angelina.'

'Not me, Mr Wolfe, Momma Gabrielle she done fixed you up. She say it a good job she got to you afore the arm gone rotten.'

He looked at her for a moment. 'Momma Gabrielle – where the hell are we?'

'Snakebite Junction – when the railroad men told us they was gonna fire the house we had nowhere to go. It were Tobias as brought us here.'

'Tell me what happened.'

So she told him about the raid and the shooting of her husband. 'So we loaded Miss Lavinia on the wagon along with my poor dead Seth and came here.' Tears ran down her cheeks as she spoke.

'Lavinia – she here too? You mean she was thrown out of her own house?'

Before Angelina could answer the door opened and an extremely beautiful black woman entered.

'So Mr Wolfe is awake. That is good. How is the mighty warrior?'

Zacchaeus stared up at the woman and, in spite of his pain and distress, was somewhat stirred by her beauty. He was looking for a touch of irony in her expression. Gracefully she moved to the bed, reached out a slim hand and rested it on his forehead. She nodded.

'The fever is gone. You will need rest and nourishment to recover fully.'

'Send Lavinia to me, I want to talk to her.'

Momma Gabrielle stared soberly at the man in the bed. Slowly she sank down on to the side of the bed. 'You don't know about your niece, do you?'

He shook his head. 'What is it I don't know?'

'They tell me you were in prison, Mr Wolfe. I take it you got no news from the outside world?'

Again he shook his head.

'I will tell you what I know. It is what I learned from Tobias and Angelina. While you were away your niece's fiancé was murdered. Your nephews, Marty and Murdock were hanged for the murder. Their brother Lucius attempted to save them and several soldiers were killed during the rescue attempt. Now he is on the run with a price on his head.

'Your niece, Lavinia was found brutally beaten and left for dead. No one knows who did this to her. I have done what I can for her but the wounds are so severe she is insensible of this world.' She reached out and took his good hand. 'I am sorry. This great curse that has befallen your family has touched you as well and taken your hand.'

He looked down at his neatly bandaged stump. 'Lavinia,' he whispered. 'Not Lavinia! And I wasn't there to protect her. Lavinia. . . .' His voice broke and it was several moments before he could speak again. 'My nephews murdered – my niece lying at death's door – my good friend Seth slain – the ranch taken over by thieves . . . Leave me . . . leave me to my grief and my black thoughts. When I am ready I will come and look upon my niece.'

'Eat your broth, Mr Wolfe,' Angelina pleaded but he ignored her – his face set in a bleak mask of anguish. The two women, not knowing how to console him, rose and quietly left the room.

Later in the day Tobias came in to the room and found him in that same, tormented state.

'Mr Wolfe, is there anything I can do?'

'Get me my clothes, Tobias. I must go to my niece.'

Tobias helped him dress and guided him to the room where Lavinia was confined. Momma Gabrielle followed them, as did Angelina.

Zacchaeus sat on the edge of the bed and stared at his niece. Her face had lost the corpselike look but she was still very pale. He reached out and took her limp hand in his remaining one. She opened her eyes and looked out at him.

'Lavinia,' he whispered, 'it is your Uncle Zac come to see you.'

She opened her mouth as if to speak but no sound came out.

'Speak to me, Lavinia, tell me who attacked you?'

Momma Gabrielle moved to the other side of the bed and gently pulled down the high neck of the nightdress.

The brutal gash had been sewn neatly along its length but the wound was still red and puckered. Zacchaeus stared in horror at the dreadful injury.

'Lavinia, who did this terrible thing?'

'She cannot speak – her throat was so badly damaged.'

Zacchaeus switched his eyes from the girl to the tall elegant woman on the other side of the bed. 'Will she recover?'

Momma Gabrielle shrugged her shoulders, her beautiful face revealing her sorrow at the girl's plight. She could not put into words her feelings but he could see plainly her distress. He looked again at the appalling scar on the girl's neck. Slowly he reached out and stroked her pale cheek.

'Lavinia, when you are well enough you will tell me who did this to you. When I heard of your brothers' fate I thought I could bear no more sorrow but I see there will be no peace in this world while the vile people who wrought all these woes upon us are unpunished. I swear to you now, Lavinia, you will be avenged. I swear to you.'

He felt a gentle touch on his arm. 'Mr Wolfe, do not let vengeance poison your life. You have tasted enough unhappiness. You have lost loved ones and your body has suffered much. Let your life become one dedicated to peace and caring for your niece. She will need someone to look after her.'

He looked at Momma Gabrielle and she recoiled at the expression in his eyes. 'I am not much good at peace. I thought I was. When the war ended I hung up my weapons and was settling down to run my ranch with the help of my nephews and my faithful cowhands, Tobias and Seth. I was building for my brother's boys. Now they are dead or exiled and my niece . . .' he gazed down at the girl in the bed, '. . . my niece might as well be dead.

'These people declared war on me and mine. Her life

and the lives of her brothers have been destroyed. Can I run from that? So don't talk to me of peace. My life is no longer my own. I am an instrument of vengeance. I will find these people, should it take the rest of my life. They shall feel the full wrath of Zacchaeus Wolfe.'

'Mr Wolfe.' The big blacksmith nodded to Zacchaeus. 'You feeling better?'

'Somewhat,' Zacchaeus replied, his tone noncommittal. He looked critically around the workshop. 'Ain't much work for a blacksmith round here.'

The big man shrugged. 'I get along. Make barrel-hoops and take them in to Salem from time to time. The brewery buys them.'

Zacchaeus nodded. 'Roland, I need some work doing.'

'Sure thing, I is a wizard with ironwork.' The blacksmith stared levelly at his customer. 'One thing I wanna ask you. I hope you don't take offence. It's more to satisfy my own curiosity.'

Zacchaeus waited patiently.

'You that Zacchaeus Wolfe – I mean the one as rode with the Grey Wolves?'

Zacchaeus turned and looked back out into the street. It was mid-morning and the town was stirring to life. A weak sun shone into the workshop. 'I guess so. Does it bother you?'

'I worked on a ranch up in Jason County. We was raising beef for the Union troops. The man as owned me was a mean bastard. For the smallest misdemeanour we were whipped. One day he took my woman, Joanna, and sold her just to spite me. I guess I kinda went a bit mad then. I did my best to kill him. He had me tied to a post and was about to flog me when the Grey Wolves rode up to the ranch. They told my master they was requisitioning the cattle for they own troops. The man in charge of those

Grey Wolves had me cut down and had my master tied to the post in place of me. They rounded up the cattle and drove them away leaving me with a whip in my hand and my old master tied up to that there post.'

The big man ceased speaking and Zacchaeus was still staring out into the roadway.

'I never used that there whip. I threw it from me and walked away from that ranch. No one stopped me. I just walked away and only stopped walking when I got here. I been here ever since.'

By now Zacchaeus had turned around to face the black-smith. 'Where did you learn to work a smithy?'

'On that ranch – horseshoes, wheel-rims, gate-hinges shovels, picks. I made all the tools as was used around the place. Neighbouring farmers and ranchers brought in work as well – broken farm machinery, harness for repair. There weren't nothing I couldn't put my hand to.'

Zacchaeus held up his stump. It had healed well in the intervening weeks but he kept it wrapped in a muslin sleeve. 'I need a weapon.'

For a moment or two the blacksmith stared at the stump. 'What you have in mind – a club or a blade?'

'A blade would be too obvious. A steel cap could be disguised.'

'Once a gambling man came by here. He ask me could I repair his boots. He didn't want them soled or heeled. Inside the toecap was a spring-loaded blade. When he was in a fight this blade came in handy, being as it was mostly hid in the boot till he needed it.'

'A spring-loaded blade.' Zacchaeus looked speculatively at the speaker. 'You reckon you could do something simi-lar for a missing hand?'

'You supply the blade. I'll make it fit.'

'I'll get the blade.'

'Mr Wolfe.'

Zacchaeus was turning to leave. He stopped and turned back again.

'There won't be no charge for any of this. I reckon I have a debt to repay.'

'I understand, Roland. I just wish I had your courage.'

'My courage – what the hell you mean?'

'You threw away that whip. It took a big man to do that. I could never have thrown away the whip. I am too mean for such generous behaviour.'

25

Tamara came to the door and stared at the large body of horsemen pouring into the yard. A buggy rolled up and stopped opposite the steps. She stared in surprise as Samuel Eldridge grinned at her from the passenger seat. He jumped down and came round to the steps.

'Get my stuff unloaded and packed away,' he called to the driver. 'You men,' he yelled to the riders, 'find stabling and quarters. You may have to rough it for a bit till we get things arranged.'

'Samuel, what a surprise! What's happening?'

He wrapped his arms around her and kissed her fervently. 'I'm moving in here with you.'

'Oh, Samuel, this is so sudden. You should have let me know. The place is such a mess.'

'Any place is heaven with you, my darling,' he quipped and then his face sobered. 'I figure we're all safer together where the Pinkerton men can keep an eye on us.' He indicated the horsemen now disappearing round the back of the house. 'That goddamn Lucius Wolfe has been robbing and killing all along the railroad. He's gathered a gang of bandits around him and each time he raids a pay-wagon or an office he leaves a note for me. Says he's coming for me. He musta heard about you and the boys living out here, for he now includes threats against you and your family.'

A worried frown appeared on her handsome face. 'You

128

mean to stay here permanent?'

'Sure thing, honey. Did you miss me? for I sure as hell missed you!'

'Oh Samuel, this is wonderful. Go you in the parlour and I'll fix us some drinks.'

She waited for Samuel to disappear through the door and then turned and ran upstairs. Aaron was lying on the bed when she flung open the door. 'Get your things and get the hell outta here,' she said frantically. 'Samuel's downstairs. He reckons he's come to stay.'

Aaron smiled his golden-toothed smile. 'What the hell! Tell him you're spoken for.'

'Damn it, Aaron, don't spoil things. We have a nice little thing going here. I have to get hold of the deeds of this place and then you can tell him yourself. Just do as I say. If Samuel finds you here there'll be hell to pay. Now shift your ass. I'll keep him occupied while you move out.'

With ill-grace the gunman began to gather his belongings while Tamara returned to an impatient Samuel.

'You are still very weak, Mr Wolfe, I hope you are not riding far.'

Zacchaeus finished tying his mount to the front of the hotel and turned to look at the beautiful black woman quizzing him. 'I am riding into Salem. My brother has certain things of mine. He was keeping them for me.' He mounted the steps and she stood aside to let him enter. 'I want to see my niece before I leave. If I tell her I am going to see her father it might stimulate some reaction.'

She followed him into Lavinia's bedroom. Angelina was sitting on a chair reading to her.

'Lavinia, I am riding into Salem to see your father. Is there any message for him?'

The girl's eyes opened and she stared up at him. Zacchaeus was moved to sit on the bed.

129

'It breaks my heart to see you like this, Lavinia. One day I will find out who did this terrible thing to you and when I do they will pay the ultimate price.'

Her mouth opened and closed and her lips formed words but no sound was emitted. Large tears rolled down her cheeks. Zacchaeus looked round for something to wipe away the tears. Angelina closed her book and handed him a handkerchief As he took it he stared intently at the book. 'Momma Gabrielle,' he said urgently, 'have you got a pencil and paper?'

'Yeah.'

She retrieved a notebook and a graphite pencil and handed it to him. He in turn handed the items to the girl in the bed.

'Write, Lavinia, write what happened.' His voice was low and urgent.

Her eyes darted to the items he had handed to her. With sudden urgency she began to write. The silence in the room was so intense the scratching of the pencil on the paper sounded like the urgent scraping of an animal clawing at its prison in a frantic attempt to escape.

He kept the glasses on the house, counting the riders and noting their weapons. All carried carbines and side-arms. They filed round the back of the house out of sight and he presumed they were off-saddling and corralling their mounts. He recognized Samuel and Tamara. They disappeared inside and though he waited another hour they did not reappear. He stowed the glasses in the saddle-bags and mounted. Skirting well round the ranch he headed for town. He was dressed in buckskin shirt and leather leggings like countless other cowboys. A borrowed Colt was pushed inside his coat. He anticipated no trouble and wanted none. His appointment was with his brother.

Reverend Makepeace Wolfe heard the footsteps on the porch and waited for the knock on the door. None came. He went back to writing his sermon for Sunday service. His study door opened and he looked up with some annoyance. He sat there staring at the figure in the doorway.

Zacchaeus eased inside the room. He kept his eyes steady on his brother.

'Zacchaeus, where did you come from? I . . . I thought you were dead or imprisoned. The military wouldn't tell me anything. Not that I blame them after what Lucius did. What happened? Did they release you?'

Zacchaeus walked further inside the room. 'It matters little what happened to me. As far as the military is concerned I am probably dead or lost amongst the paperwork. I'd rather they keep on thinking that.'

The preacher's eyes widened. 'Are you a fugitive? For God's sake, Zacchaeus, give yourself up. This family has caused enough trouble. Lucius is running with some wild gang and has a price on his head. He tried to rescue Marty and Murdock and a lot of blood was shed. And . . . and Lavinia . . . I don't know what has happened to Lavinia. One moment she was at the ranch and then when I went to visit she had disappeared and that scarlet woman was living there.' He stared with agonied eyes at the grim figure standing before him. 'What sins have we committed to bring such sorrow upon our heads, Zacchaeus?'

'We have committed no sins, Makepeace. We have been grievously sinned against.' He took a notepad from his pocket and after opening it handed it to the preacher.

'Read that, brother. Read it out loud.'

'On the day my father invited my beloved Barnabas and his brother Samuel on a hunting trip Tamara came to me at the house. She told me Barnabas was in an accident and begged me to go with her. She led

131

me to the old shack up near the mines where shepherds used to stay when the sheep were lambing. Inside was not my Barnabas but her two evil sons, Demetrius and Keiren. Before she left me with them she told me that Aaron was to kill my beloved Barnabas and blame it on my brothers.'

Makepeace stopped reading and stared at Zacchaeus. 'Did Lavina write this?'

'Read on brother, do not spare yourself. Read on.'

'Those two fiends then attacked me. They committed the most vile acts on my body and then clubbed me into unconsciousness.

Makepeace stopped again.
'Read on brother.'

'Uncle Zac, when you have revenged these acts you will come back and tell me that vile family are all dead. Then I beg of you to take my life. For this existence is a living hell.'

Makepeace stared at Zacchaeus. 'Where is she, brother? She must be recovering if she was able to write this.'

'She is in a safe place for now. It is best no one knows where she is or even that she is still alive. The people who did that to her will want her dead. I will take you to her if you like.'

'I . . . I can't leave, Zacchaeus. I have much to do here. The Lord's work is onerous. I must fight the good fight against the sins and depravity that I see all around me.'

The brothers stared at each other for some moments.

'As you will, Makepeace,' Zacchaeus said at last. 'You have something of mine that I need.'

'You have only to ask me, Zacchaeus. What is it you require?'

'When I returned from the war I left my guns and knives with you. I need them again.'

Makepeace stared in consternation at his brother. 'But the oath, you swore an oath never to take up arms again. You cannot break an oath. You swore on this Holy Bible.' The preacher placed his hand on the Bible lying open on the desk.

'I remember it well, brother Makepeace. I remember every word of that oath. *I, Zacchaeus Wolfe, swear on the family Bible held by my brother the Reverend Makepeace Wolfe that from this day henceforth this hand will never pull a weapon on another fellow being. As God and Reverend Makepeace Wolfe are my witness.*'

'Oh, thank God, brother. We will find redemption for you yet. Let us kneel and pray. Then I shall take this testament written by Lavinia to the authorities and they will prosecute the vile creatures that committed these heinous crimes against my family.'

Zacchaeus stood regarding his brother, no expression in his dark eyes. 'Have you learned nothing, Makepeace, after all that has happened? There will be no justice from that quarter, brother. We must administer our own justice. I shall fetch my weapons.'

'The oath . . . Zacchaeus . . . you can't go against your oath!'

The Reverend Makepeace Wolfe stared in puzzlement as his brother held up his arm. Slowly he pulled away a muslin sleeve that had kept it covered.

'That is the hand that I swore with. *This hand will never pull a weapon on another fellow being.* God released me from my oath, Makepeace. God took my hand. The oath is null and void.'

26

'Where's Tobias, Angelina, I need to speak with him.'

Zacchaeus was standing beside Lavinia's bed.

'He's gone, Master Zacchaeus, he said he was gonna search out Master Lucius and ask him what's to be done about Miss Lavinia.'

'I told her father,' Zaccheus mused, 'but he ain't turned up.'

Zacchaeus turned as Momma Gabrielle came into the room.

'I need a duster coat. Can you find me one?'

'I seen Roland wearing one: he might be persuaded to lend it.'

'I'll wander that way and ask.'

'I'll walk with you.'

Zacchaeus and Momma Gabrielle walked together. The street was muddy. Up till now, no one in Snakebite had thought it important to lay boardwalks. Roland was hammering on a barrel-hoop when they entered.

'A duster?' The big black man looked speculatively at Zacchaeus, then walked to an inner room to retrieve the item. He was grinning widely when he handed the rust-coloured coat over.

'What's so funny?'

When Zacchaeus donned the coat it trailed on the ground and the sleeves were so long it looked as if there were no arms inside. Roland burst out laughing and Momma Gabrielle giggled delightfully.

'You could hire yourself out as a bird-scarer, Zacchaeus,' the big man remarked between chuckles.

'I'll pin it up for you,' Momma Gabrielle said, moving over. She began to roll back the sleeves. Her eyes were full of amusement as she looked at him. Suddenly she sobered and bent her head.

'It'll be dark anyway when I'm wearing it,' Zacchaeus said, wondering what it was that he saw in the woman's eyes.

'I got that equipment ready, Zacchaeus.'

'Show me.'

Roland brought him an object that had all the appearance of a cannon shell. It was formed of round dull metal with leather straps dangling. Zacchaeus shrugged off the oversize coat and presented his mutilated limb. Deftly the blacksmith strapped the object in place. He pointed to a small trigger. 'When you push that it operates the blade, but be careful – it has a vicious spring.' He pressed the lever and with an audible click a slim, lethal blade shot into view. 'You'll need a mighty effort to get it back in again. I have made a metal plate that attaches to your cartridge belt. Use that to depress the blade.'

Zacchaeus regarded his new extension. 'This is a formidable weapon, Roland. I might kill someone with such a vicious device.'

Roland returned to his hoop-making. 'Good luck, Zacchaeus, take good care of my coat.'

As he was saddling up she walked out to him and stood watching. 'Do you have to go, Zacchaeus?'

He turned and looked at her. She was extremely beautiful, dressed in a crimson, high-necked cotton blouse and long, pleated skirt.

'It is my fate.'

'We make our own fate, Zacchaeus.'

He regarded her soberly. 'I am a killer. The war fashioned me thus. And since the war, coyotes have savaged my family and stolen my land. The only way to protect what remains is to wipe out the vermin that have infested my life.'

'Zacchaeus, I have been curious about you since you and your family came here. You are a strong man and you are a good man. I've seen you with your niece. No one could be more gentle or more caring. Roland told me of his encounter with you when you rescued him. I have waited for such a man all my life. Stay here with me. Forget the vengeance. Forget the killing. We could make a life here. I could make you happy. There is a loneliness in us both. We will be good for each other.'

He stared at her too surprised to speak. 'In all my life,' he said eventually, his voice filled with emotion, 'no one has ever paid me such a compliment.' He raised his stump – the brutal metal now sheathed in a thin leather cover, and regarded it for a moment. 'We just fought a war to abolish the slave trade. This is Virginia, I am a white man and you are a black woman. I know you are a free woman but somehow I don't think people here are ready for to tolerate such a union.'

For answer she produced a folded sheet of paper and after straightening it out handed it to him.

'Millions of acres,' he read aloud, 'Iowa and Nebraska lands, for sale on ten years' credit. Burlington and Missouri River company.' He raised his head and gazed at her standing there with a hand covering her mouth and looking back at him with her large, expressive eyes.

'Out there no one would care about colour. We could make a fresh start. It's a dream I have, to run a farm or ranch with a strong man by my side.'

'You need a good man, Gabrielle. Not someone as is crippled in mind and body.'

'I will heal you, Zacchaeus Wolfe. And you are a good man no matter what you say. The men you go after are evil. Them as did that to Lavinia are evil. You're not like them. You are honourable and compassionate and you want to see justice meted out. The law of the land won't punish the evildoers so you are forced to take the law into your own hands. That's what makes you strong. You are not afraid to believe in your own just cause.'

He kept his gaze on her. 'I may not return,' he said at last. 'Formidable odds are gathered at my old home. Pinkerton agents patrol the grounds day and night protecting the house.' He indicated the duster. 'They all wear these, I thought it would get me close.'

She stepped forward and put her arms around his neck. Her lips crushed against his. When she released him his eyes held the startled look of a man who has just had a glimpse of paradise. Wonderingly he put his hand up and touched his lips. Then he turned and climbed on to his horse. Without a backward glance he heeled his mount and moved up the street.

'You come back, Zacchaeus Wolfe, you hear me. We got plans, you and me.'

She watched him disappear into the distance with tear-bright eyes.

27

Farley McKenna sat his mount and stared into the night. Sighing deeply he pulled out his tobacco-sack and began to roll himself a smoke.

'What the goddamn hell I'm supposed to be on the look-out for, I sure as hell don't know,' he muttered as he concentrated on his cigarette. He licked the paper and applied a sulphur-head. 'That Lucius Wolfe only attacks mail trains and banks belonging to Southern Railroad. Why he would want to bother coming here to this god-forsaken place beats me.'

He sat his mount quietly, smoking and thinking of the easy time he and his Pinkerton buddies had in Salem. On their nights off they could drink and gamble and whore in the saloons that catered for red-blooded men. Now they had to spend their nights in a crowded bunkhouse full of men just as frustrated and bored as he was.

A rider appeared out of the darkness. He frowned as he watched the man draw near. Fed up and feeling facetious he decided to have a bit of light-hearted fun. 'Friend or foe,' he suddenly called out.

'What the hell you think, you dumb asshole?' came the reply.

Farley grinned in the dark, pleased to have riled the rider. He couldn't quite make out the man approaching but he knew it was one of the Pinkerton men, for his long duster hung each side of his mount. 'What the hell you doing? You can't be my relief. I'm out here till midnight.'

'Saw your light. I ain't got no matches.'

The sentry reached for his makings again. By now the rider was almost level. He leaned forward as if reaching for the matches. The hand swept up and something hard and blunt hit Farley on the nose with such force it crushed the cartilage flat against his face. The instant shock and pain were blinding. As he reeled back there came another fierce, bone-crushing blow to his temple and Farley McKenna toppled from his horse.

His attacker grabbed the bridle of the fallen man's horse. 'Whoa there, fella.' He slid down off his own horse, led the captured mount further into the brush and tethered both animals. Then he returned and dragged the unfortunate sentry so that he too was concealed. He proceeded on foot in the direction of the house.

As he crouched in the shadows he could hear music. Zacchaeus Wolfe grinned into the darkness.

'Play, my friends. I'm coming in to join the party.'

He rose up and walked towards the rear of the house. A dark figure loomed out of the night. Zacchaeus could see the rifle barrel as the man pointed it towards him.

'Who the hell's that,' a rough voice growled.

'Tom, damn horse spooked and threw me. I think it was a wolf or something.'

'Tom, Tom Shelby. . . ?' the man with the rifle queried uncertainly.

Zacchaeus saw the rifle barrel dip. He moved swiftly, driving a long-bladed Bowie into the man's throat. They both fell to the ground and rolled into shadow. As the man died beneath him Zacchaeus was scanning the yard.

'What the hell's going on over there?'

Another guard stepped out from the barn, peering over at the disturbance. Zacchaeus cursed softly but stayed where he was. His victim ceased to struggle, the blood from his ruptured throat soaking into the yard dirt.

'I think it was a goddamn rat. I can't stand rats. I tried to club it with my rifle,' he called. 'Anyway, I'm gonna take me a break.'

He took the dead man's rifle, stood upright and began walking towards the back of the house. The guard watched him go but did not challenge any further. Zacchaeus turned the corner and saw another guard lounging by the back door. The man glanced at him but perceived no threat.

'What the hell's Charlie yelling about?'

'Aw, he's just edgy,' Zacchaeus replied and swung the rifle. The guard was taken completely unawares. The barrel hit him square on his Adam's apple. He slowly knelt down, making horrible gargling noises as he gagged for breath. Again the rifle rose and fell and the man died as his skull caved in.

Zacchaeus rolled the body underneath the veranda. He stood on the boards of the back veranda and his eyes scanned his surroundings. Nothing he could see suggested he had been observed. Behind him, from the house, the music continued.

Zacchaeus drew his Colt. It was the one he had carried throughout the war. It was also the one that had killed Tamara's sons when they threatened Conway the trader and his daughters. Then he pushed open the back door and stepped inside his home.

A hallway ran towards the front of the house with doors opening into the various rooms. The floor had been newly carpeted and treading softly the intruder walked slowly, pausing to listen at every door. Suddenly he stopped and placed his ear against one particular door. He frowned as he listened. He could hear an irregular clicking and some voices and laughter.

'Billiards,' he breathed as realization came to him. He pushed the Colt inside his holster, reached out and gripped the doorknob.

Tamara looked stunning, dressed in a velvet green dress. Her flaming red hair was greatly enhanced by the green emerald tiara she wore. The neckline of the dress plunged well below what would have been acceptable in the respectable parlours of Salem. Out here in the Wolfe ranch she had no one to consider but Samuel Eldridge.

Candelabras lit up the table which was set with silverware. Glistening ice-buckets stood upon the starched white tablecloth, holding corked bottles of champagne. Several places were set for dinner. By the large fireplace a pianola played a lively tune into the candlelit room. In the centre of the room the couple swayed and danced to the music.

'Tamara, I shall never forget our stay here. These have been the happiest days of my life. It was an inspired plan when you suggested taking over this house. I feel safer here than I did in town. This place is so easy to guard. There's Pinkerton men riding patrol around the grounds and men standing guard front and back of the house. If that Lucius Wolfe tries to get anywhere near here he'll be shot to pieces before he gets within a hundred yards of the place.'

'Tut, tut, darling, forget about that horrible Lucius Wolfe. He's an outlaw with a price on his head. Sooner or later someone will turn him in. Now, this is your birthday and I've gone to great bother to make it special for you. You're going to have a night to remember. So no more talk of that horrible Wolfe family. Enjoy yourself!'

'You're the best birthday present I could have. In fact I have a special surprise for you.'

'Oh, Samuel, you give me too much already. I don't deserve any more gifts.'

141

'This one is special.' He groped in a waistcoat pocket and produced a small velvet-covered box. With slow deliberate movements he flicked open the lid and exposed the contents to her. She gasped in astonishment and pleasure.

'Samuel, oh, Samuel, it is so beautiful!'

'It's an engagement ring, Tamara.' Suddenly he knelt before her. 'Tamara, I have thought long and hard about this. I wanted to be sure you felt about me as I felt about you. Tamara, will you do me the honour of becoming my wife?'

'Samuel,' she squealed and pulled him to his feet. She flung her arms round him and held him tight. 'This is the happiest day of my life. I will be proud to marry you. I love you so much.'

28

Two large kerosene lamps hung over the table, throwing bright illumination onto the green baize. So engrossed were the two youths that neither of them looked up as the door opened and Zacchaeus slipped inside the room.

'Hush.' Demetrius hissed a warning to the intruder as he bent over the cue lining up his target. His brother leaned against the corner of the billiard-table with the butt of his cue resting upon the floor, intently observing the play. On the rim of the table lay coins and dollar bills, evidence of wagers being placed on the outcome of the game.

Zacchaeus obeyed the warning to be quiet and edged silently around the youths. He stopped behind Demetrius with Keiren to his right and waited patiently for the cue stroke to be played.

'Yes!' enthused Demetrius as the red ball cannoned into the side pocket. He was still crouched over the table, eyeing up his next shot when Zacchaeus moved. The metal mitt came smashing down on the back of the youth's head. Zacchaeus did not use his full force with the blow but nevertheless the youth's face slammed into the table with sufficient force to break his nose. He hung there helpless with shock and pain, not out, but dazed by the force and suddenness of the assault.

Even as Keiren whirled to confront the attacker

Zacchaeus grabbed up the cue his brother had dropped on the table and swung it with brutal force against the youth's mouth. Keiren screamed as the polished wooden cue smashed teeth and crushed his lips. He staggered back trying to bring his own cue up to ward off his attacker. Using the cue like a javelin Zacchaeus rammed the blunt end hard into the already bleeding mouth. Kieren's screams were abruptly cut off. He sprawled heavily to the floor and clamped his hands to his ruined mouth. As he lay there, mewling with pain and terror, blood poured from his mouth on to his hands and down on to his shirt.

Still holding the cue Zacchaeus hooked a chair towards him with his foot and sat down. Calmly he observed the two injured youths.

Demetrius moaned and opened his eyes. He was lying half-on and half-off the table. Blood had pooled on the table top from his broken nose. He blinked a few times and pushed himself upright. 'Wha . . . what happened?'

He could not see his brother but could hear the moaning of his injured sibling. Neither could he see Zacchaeus, who was sitting quietly behind him. He straightened up and with unsteady movements came round the corner of the table to see his brother curled up on the floor vainly trying to stem the pain and blood welling from his broken mouth.

'Keiren. . . .' Realization came slowly and he turned to stare at Zacchaeus.

The man who had attacked them so suddenly and so brutally still held the billiard-cue. He was sitting relaxed and seemingly at ease, calmly watching them. There was no expression on that hard, honed face.

'You. . . .' Recognition registered in Demetrius's face and fear took him so he could only gape at the apparition and hold on to the table for support.

'Howdy, Demetrius, or is it Keiren? It doesn't really

matter,' Zacchaeus began conversationally. 'This used to be my home. My nephews stayed here with me and helped me run the ranch. Lavinia, she also stayed here occasionally. You remember Lavinia – lovely dark hair and exquisite features. She had the most wonderful smile and loved baking. All gone now – only strangers living in the old Wolfe household.' He cocked his head. 'I hear music. Is it a party, or what?'

As Zacchaeus talked Demetrius had started trembling. His eyes were starting wide with terror. He made no reply to the intruder's question. Zacchaeus hefted the cue and made as if to hit the youth again. Demetrius flinched and cowered back. The cue hit him on the ear. He yelled out and crouched down by the side of the table, holding his hands out in a vain attempt to ward off the terrible nemesis that had crashed into their life with such violence.

'Please don't hit me any more,' he pleaded. 'I'll do whatever you ask.'

'When I ask a question you will answer immediately. I need to know who is in the house and what rooms they are in.'

'Ma and Samuel are up in the dining-room. That's where the music is coming from. It's Samuel's birthday. They're having a birthday dinner to celebrate. Cook's preparing dinner now. Soon they'll call us to eat.'

Zacchaeus glanced at the door. 'Who will come for you? Will it be the cook?'

'We have a dinner-gong. Ma or Samuel will ring that and Keiren and me will join them.'

Zacchaeus thought about this for a moment. 'Where's Aaron,' he asked suddenly.

The youth shrugged. 'I don't know. He hasta keep outta the way when Samuel's here. He bunks out with the Pinkerton men.'

Zacchaeus fell silent. He was remembering the last visit here. He had been half-delirious with pain and exhaustion. When he'd entered the house a man and a woman were engaged in lovemaking on the settee. Suddenly he knew who that man and woman were. He frowned as he remembered that night.

'I thought Tamara and Samuel were lovers.'

The youth's eyes slid sideways and he did not answer. Zacchaeus sighed.

'Let's get you two ready for dinner. I don't want to disappoint your ma.'

He stood and looked around the room. A large cotton sheet lay crumpled on a chair. It was obviously the cover for the billiard-table. He laid the cue on the floor and took out his Bowie. The youth's eyes opened wide as he saw the long-bladed instrument.

'What you gonna do, mister? Don't kill us. We don't mean you no harm.'

Zacchaeus ignored him and began to carve strips from the sheet. He tossed one of these to the terrified youth.

'Use that to gag your brother. If you don't do a good job I'll slice away your ears.'

He watched as the youth did as he was told. Keiren moaned piteously as the gag dug into his ruined mouth. Quickly it took on the colour of blood.

'Now tie his hands behind his back.'

When this task was completed to his satisfaction Zacchaeus ordered the thoroughly cowed youth to bend over on the billiard-table in the position he had been when Zacchaeus had first entered. Whimpering fearfully he did as he was told. Zacchaeus gagged him and tied his hands behind him. Then he went back to his chair and sat there waiting and listening to the distant sound of music coming from the dining-room. He sat there, a terrible and silent spectre of retribution.

His victims suffered and wept into their gags, unable to stifle the sobs of fear and pain so suddenly and brutally inflicted upon their luxurious and pleasurable life styles.

29

The dinner gong tolled like a funeral bell summoning the mourners to the feast. The two youths glanced fearfully at the man who had disabled them so brutally and so efficiently. Zacchaeus rose and moved to the door. Carefully he opened it and poked his head out. He watched as a man and a woman came out of the dining-room wheeling an empty serving-trolley. They trundled along the hallway and disappeared in the direction of the kitchen.

'OK, boys, time to party.'

They walked ahead of him. He was trying to watch the hallway behind him as well as up front as he escorted his prisoners towards the front of the house. The little party arrived at the dining-room without incident. Zacchaeus pushed open the door into the dining-room and ushered his victims inside.

Tamara turned towards them with a glass of wine in her hand. The smile froze on her face as she stared at the appalling sight of her sons with bloody rags bound across their mouths. Zacchaeus pushed the door to behind him and pulled out his Colt.

'Evening, everyone! Oh yes – happy birthday, Samuel.'

Samuel had his back to the door. He had been busy filling wine-glasses. He whirled and stared at the gruesome trio. Zacchaeus waved his long-barrelled Colt in the air. 'Don't do anything foolish, either of you.' Moving in behind the two blood-splattered youths he ordered them to kneel. They did as they were told, beginning to sob again at the sight of their mother.

Zacchaeus walked forward. 'Sit,' he ordered the bewildered couple.

Tamara turned hate-filled eyes to him. 'What have you done to my boys?' she hissed. 'You're a dead man for this.'

Zacchaeus nodded amiably. 'People often tell me that.'

He prodded the exposed flesh of her plunging neckline with the barrel of his Colt, forcing her to sit. Then he motioned to Samuel to do the same. Only when the couple were seated did he give his attention to the lavish spread upon the table.

'Sucking pig.' He nodded approvingly. 'Roast turkey, and that looks like cranberry sauce, excellent. Ah yes, my favourite, roast potatoes.'

He holstered his Colt and picked up a large carving knife. Leaning across the table he deftly sliced away at one of the turkey platters. Holding the knife and the turkey leg in his one good hand he was about to bite into the flesh when he paused.

'But you're not eating! Eat up. It all looks delicious.'

The man and woman stared up at him with the look of trapped animals. The woman's eyes were filled with hate while Samuel's face was filled with both fear and loathing. They made no move towards the food before them. What had been a happy occasion of celebration had turned into a feast of terror.

'Oh, I know what's wrong, you haven't said grace.' He laid the carving-knife and his turkey on the table, and fished in his pocket and produced a notebook.

'Here, Samuel, read from this. It's not the same as a

religious script but it's quite interesting.' He placed the opened book in front of Samuel and picked up his knife and turkey. 'Go on, read,' he urged. With the speed of a striking snake he struck. Tamara screamed as the knife carved a bloody gash across her hand. A derringer tumbled on to the table and the woman fell back in her chair clutching her bleeding hand and staring with malevolent, pain-filled eyes at her tormentor. Zacchaeus hooked the point of the knife into the trigger-guard of the small pistol and slipped it into his pocket.

'Don't interrupt again,' Zacchaeus said sternly. He turned and pushed the knife hard into Samuel's cheek. A trickle of blood ran down his face to drip from his chin. 'Now read.'

In a quavering voice Samuel began to read.

'On the day my father invited my beloved Barnabas and his brother Samuel on a hunting trip Tamara came to me at the house. She told me Barnabas was in an accident and begged me to go with her. She led me to the old mine shack where the shepherds used to stay when the sheep were lambing. Inside was not my Barnabas but her two evil sons, Demetrius and Keiren. Before she left me with them she told me that Aaron was to kill my beloved Barnabas and blame it on my brothers.'

Samuel raised his head and looked up at Zacchaeus. 'What is this? None of this can be true,' he asked of the grim figure.

By now Zacchaeus had walked across the room and was standing beside the two sobbing youths.

'Read on, friend. You are as much a victim in this evil plan as was my family.'

'Those two fiends then attacked me. They committed the most vile acts on my body and then beat me around the head till I knew no more.'

When he finished reading Samuel turned to the woman sitting at the table with him. 'None of it is true, Tamara,' he said, his voice trembling, 'tell me none of this is true.'

She said nothing, staring at her enemy now standing by her sons.

'You don't expect the truth from her now do you, Samuel? The last time I called here, she and her pet gunslinger, Aaron, were frolicking together in the front room.' Zacchaeus shook his head in mock reprimand. 'Shocking behaviour.'

'He's lying, Samuel. Can't you see he's trying to provoke us?'

'What are these creatures' names, Tamara?' asked Zacchaeus, pointing with the carving knife at Demetrius.

'You know very well they are my sons, Demetrius and Keiren. You murdered my other boys.'

Zacchaeus shook his head. 'Wrong! This one is Rape!' With brutal suddenness he dragged the carving knife across the youth's neck. He fell sideways trying to scream through his gag as the blood from the terrible cut in his throat pumped on to the carpet. 'And this one is Murder!' Again that terrible slashing movement and the second youth was twitching out his life on the floor.

Tamara was on her feet, screaming. Samuel had pushed back his chair with a horrified look on his face. They were both staring towards him with terror and fear in their faces.

If Tamara had not been screaming – and as it was she increased the intensity of her screams – Zacchaeus might have heard the door open behind him. He might even have seen some expression on the faces of his enemies that would have warned him. As it was something smashed into the back of his head without warning and he pitched forward on to the bodies of the youths whose lives he had so brutally terminated.

30

He could smell blood. It was strong and in his nostrils. During the war the smell had become familiar to him along with other obnoxious odours such as decaying corpses or the acrid smell of cordite. Now the smell of blood was immediate in his nose. He could hear voices and he lay still and listened. Beside him the bodies of his victims smelt of death and blood.

'Kill him, Aaron. Slit his throat like he did my poor boys. Oh, my God, my poor boys.' The voice was that of Tamara, grieving for her dead children.

'Not yet, Tamara, I have other plans for him. When I have finished with him you can have him.'

Someone kicked him in the head and the dull pain flared into agonizing sharpness. He groaned and rolled over and looked up into the face of Aaron. The man was smiling down at him, exposing golden teeth as if for Zacchaeus to admire.

'You're sure one tough son of a bitch. What happened to Sergeant McCluskey? He was supposed to finish you off.'

Zacchaeus stared up at the gunman. Aaron was holding the Colt that Zacchaeus had been carrying.

'It was the chain of events that led to his demise,' Zacchaeus replied.

Aaron shook his head. 'Get up!'

Slowly and painfully Zacchaeus got to his feet.

'Against that wall.'

Zacchaeus shuffled back to the wall as ordered.

Aaron held up Zacchaeus's Colt. 'I heard many tales of your exploits during the war. Legend had it that you were fast and deadly with this here Colt.'

Zacchaeus said nothing, watching the gunman. He was resigned to his fate. Most of what he had set out to do had been accomplished. The men who had ravished Lavinia lay dead in their own blood on the carpet while their mother had witnessed her sons receive the justice that would never have been delivered in any earthly court. He had intended to slay everyone in the room, for he held them all equally responsible for what had happened to his family. If Tamara had her way, and he did not doubt that she would, he would suffer before he died. So he awaited his fate with stoic resignation.

Aaron held up the ebony-handled Colt. Slowly and deliberately he ejected the shells, letting them drop to the carpet. The last shell he held up for Zacchaeus to observe. He inserted this back in the Colt and spun the cylinder.

'I pride myself on my speed and accuracy with a pistol, Wolfe. Never had reason to doubt I was the best. Now I have a chance to prove it.' He walked up to Zacchaeus and stood there, smiling his golden smile. 'Always wondered: were you as fast as they said you were? It was with some regret that I induced Sergeant McCluskey to kill you. I wanted you to myself.' He shook his head in bewilderment. 'How the hell you managed to best McCluskey beats me. He assured me you were chained more secure than a dancing bear in a circus.' He held up the Colt. 'You got just one bullet. I can't risk any more. You might just take it into your head to shoot up my friends before I put a bullet in you.'

'Hell, Aaron, I watched you spin the cylinder. That

goddamn bullet could be anywhere. What chance is that to give me?'

Aaron laughed as he leaned forward and tucked the Colt into Zacchaeus's empty holster. 'I always like to hedge my bets, Wolfe. Just keep pulling the trigger. The shell might come round in time. As I said you are one dangerous son of a bitch.'

There was slight metallic click. Aaron looked down, too late to anticipate the blade now slicing into his guts. He opened his mouth and gulped as the blade tore up inside him. His hands clamped on Zacchaeus as he tried to keep upright.

'Too bad you didn't last long enough, Aaron, to find out which of us was faster.'

'You . . . you. . . .'

The hands gripping Zacchaeus relaxed and Aaron began to slide downward. Before he hit the floor Zacchaeus plucked the gunman's Colt from his holster. He turned to the only other people left alive in the room. The deadly bloodstained blade protruded from the metal mitt.

'You should have invited Aaron to the party. Now he's all cut up about it.'

Samuel and Tamara stared in fascinated horror at the seemingly indestructible man now covering them with Aaron's pistol.

From outside came the thudding of feet.

'Secure the house,' someone shouted. 'Mr Eldridge, there's an intruder in the house.'

Just before the door burst open Zacchaeus strode swiftly across the room to stand behind Tamara and Samuel.

'Don't move either of you,' he warned.

The Pinkerton man in the doorway did not stand a chance as Zacchaeus shot him in the chest. He staggered back as two more took his place and began to rake the room with gunfire. The window behind Zacchaeus disintegrated as more bullets poured in from the yard. He flung himself beneath the table and stayed there, watching the door but holding his fire.

A woman screamed and he saw a body topple to the floor before him. Tamara lay a few feet from him clutching a bloody hole in her green-velvet dress. Her mouth was working but no sounds were coming. Her eyes turned to the man beneath the table. She tried to say something but instead of words blood mushroomed from her lips.

He watched from his place of shelter as Samuel threw himself down beside her. He was stroking her face and saying something to her. Her hands fell away from the bloody wound and her head lolled sideways.

'Stop shooting!' Samuel was on his knees and yelling. 'You goddamn shot Tamara! Stop shooting!'

Slowly the firing petered out. And then surprisingly it started up again. This time no bullets were coming into the house. The shooting was all outside. Zacchaeus decided to stay where he was. He reached out and jabbed Samuel with the barrel of his stolen Colt.

'In here with me, Eldridge, you're my ace in the hole. I just might be able to bargain my way out of this mess with you as hostage.'

The firing intensified and then there was much confused shouting and slowly the noise died away. Zacchaeus waited, not knowing what was happening.

'Eldridge,' a voice called from outside, 'this is Lucius Wolfe. I've come for you as I promised. You murdered my brothers, now you have to pay.'

Samuel Eldridge turned fear-ridden eyes to the man holding him prisoner. 'Tell him. Tell him how they framed those boys. You gotta tell him.'

Zacchaeus rolled out from his hiding-place. 'Why don't you tell him yourself?' Keeping an eye on the man cowering beneath the table Zacchaeus yelled out to his nephew. 'Lucius, it's me, your Uncle Zac. Come on in.'

Within moments his nephew appeared in the dining-room doorway with a Peacemaker in his hand.

'Jesus,' he swore as he surveyed the bodies strewn around the room. 'You didn't need me, Uncle Zac. You old Grey Wolf, you went and did it all by yourself!'

'I left one for you.'

Zacchaeus pointed to Samuel, who was peering out with frightened eyes at the man who had been promising to come after him and avenge the hanging of his brothers.

Lucius grinned wolfishly.

More men were coming inside the house.

'My men,' Lucius assured his uncle. 'We got to Snakebite too late. You'd already left. But damnit, you didn't need anyone.'

Zacchaeus grinned affectionately at his nephew but refrained from any comment.

'Get this piece of shit outside,' Lucius ordered the men who had followed him inside. 'He hanged my brothers so I'm gonna return the compliment.'

'No . . . I didn't know. I swear to God it was Aaron and Tamara. Tell them, Zacchaeus, tell them. . . .'

He was still screaming his innocence when the rope choked him off.

31

The wagon rumbled down the street towards the Snake River. A large black man stepped out from the smithy and stood in the roadway with a sack dangling from his big hand. The driver of the wagon called out, 'Wo-ah, there!' and hauled on the reins.

Behind the wagon Tobias, riding one horse and leading a string of a dozen more, pulled up and waited. Behind Tobias, Lucius held up his hand and his raiders bunched up beside him. Roland walked up to the wagon.

'Got a present here for you, Zacchaeus.' He plunged his hand inside the sack and pulled out an object shaped like a cannon shell with a leather harness attached.

'I already got one of them, Roland.'

Roland shook his head. 'No you ain't.' He shook the sack and the clanking of metal objects could be heard.

Lucius, curious about the delay, nudged his mount up beside the wagon to observe the encounter.

'This one's got a threaded hole.' Roland pointed to a small hole in the blunt end of the artificial mitt. 'You need to dig.' He conjured a small spade like object from the sack. 'You need to move a bale of cotton.' This time he produced a metal hook. 'Screw one of these in place and you got no excuse for not getting the job done.' He shook the sack making the contents clank together. 'There ain't nothing you can't turn your hand to.' He slung the sack into the well of the wagon, then looked up at the beautiful black woman sitting beside Zacchaeus. 'We gonna miss you, Momma Gabrielle.'

She turned her most dazzling smile on him. 'Thank you, Roland, you been a good friend.'

Angelina's face appeared between the man and woman on the wagon seat. 'Miss Lavinia wants to know what the delay is.'

'Tell her that not only has her new auntie put a bridle on her Uncle Zac but that she's just obtained a harness to go with it,' Zacchaeus replied.

Momma Gabrielle's rich laugh rang out. She punched the man beside her in the shoulder. Zacchaeus grinned at her and, nodding to the big blacksmith, set the wagon rolling. It did not halt again until the river-edge. Lucius rode up beside the wagon.

'Goodbye, Zacchaeus, Gabrielle. I wish you every happiness in your new life.'

'You sure you won't change your mind and come with us?'

'I'm a wanted man. I'll only bring danger upon you and yours. I'm depending on you looking after the last of my family.' He turned his head. 'Goodbye, Lavinia,' he called into the wagon, 'Goodbye, Angelina.' He wheeled his horse and waved at Tobias who waved back.

'Yip, yip, yip, yip,' he suddenly yelled and the band of men hanging back from the river responded in kind. The whole party swung in behind him and thundered along the bank of the river and into the distance.

Zacchaeus watched them go, then urged his team to enter the river. Half-way across he felt an arm on his.

'Zacchaeus, can you stop here?'

He frowned at Momma Gabrielle but hauled the team to a halt. 'What the hell we want to stop in the middle of a river?'

She smiled enigmatically and produced a small linen sack. Opening it she sprinkled dirt out of it over the side of the wagon. The water quickly swirled it away.

'What the hell was that all about?'

'That was dirt from the Wolfe ranch. I used it to lift the curse from you and your family.'

'Damnit, Gabrielle, you know I don't believe in that hocus-pocus. There's no such thing as magic.'

She leaned over and kissed him. 'Oh yes there is, Zacchaeus. You and I, we got magic. We got each other.'